# ETERNAL ECHOES

## A TIMELESS LOVE STORY

*BY*

*MUJAHID BAKHT*

**Hardcover** ISBN 978-1-961299-11-5
**Paperback:** ISBN 978-1-961299-12-2
**EBook:** ISBN 978-1-961299-13-9

**Publish By**
Atlas Amazon, LLC.
United States of America

# ABOUT AUTHER

## MR. MUJAHID BAKHT,

**LIFE HISTORY:-** Mr. Bakht is a mature, experienced, extremely enthusiastic, energetic, administrator and thirty-six years have proven experienced as a businessman in international marketing and public relations. Mr. Bakht is an International Real Estate Specialist, and Professional Business and Projects Consultant. He was born in Pakistan, Educated in Pakistan and USA. Presently American Citizen belongs to business-oriented family. Thirty-Seven years Resident of New York, USA.

**BUSINESS HISTORY**:- Mr. Bakht is a Founder & President of Atlas Amazon, LLC., Mr. Bakht is a business developer and multilingual business specialist in the Caribbean, South East Asia, and the Middle East emerging markets Mr. Bakht has served, met, and host many heads of the States. Also, maintain a close relationship with investors of high net worth in the USA.

**CAREER:-** Mr. Bakht has been engaged with many multinational companies in the field of international real estate investment, communication, technology, diamond, gold, mining, Pre-Feb housing, wind & solar energy, outsourcing management, and project consulting along with business partners & associates worldwide. Mr. Bakht has participated in major national and international conferences including participated in United Nations (U.N.O.) conferences.

**TRAVEL:-** Mr. Bakht is well-traveled and visited many countries around the world.

MANAGEMENT EXPERIENCE:- Thirty-Seven years of diversified experience in project consulting, marketing, and business management. As a Director of Marketing, Director of Public Relations, Director of International Affairs, Executive Vice President, President, CEO, and Chairman of many national & multinational companies, where he served previously. Mr. Bakht hired and trained many professionals as business consultants in international marketing and supervised them. Mr. Bakht is the author and publisher of multiple books.

**CERTIFICATE OF ACHIEVEMENT**; Achievement Award was presented to Mr. Bakht by Stephen Fossler for five years of continued growth and customer satisfaction from 1996 to 2001.

**HONORS MEMBER**; Madison Who's Who of Professionals, having demonstrated exemplary achievement and distinguished contributions to the business community, registered at the Library of Congress in Washington D.C. USA. (2007 & 2008)

**HONORS MEMBER;** Premiere Who's Who International,

professional business executive having demonstrated exemplary achievement and distinguished contributions to the International business community, 2008 and 2009.

**CERTIFICATES;** Certificate of Authenticity from Bill Rodham Clinton, President of the United States, and Hillary Rodham Clinton First Lady, USA. (July 20, 2000);

**CERTIFICATE OF AUTHENTICITY;** from Terence R. McAuliffe, Chairman of Democratic National Committee, Tom Dachle, Senate Democratic Leader, Dick Gephardt, House Democratic Leader, USA. (June 16, 2001);

**CERTIFICATE OF AUTHENTICITY**; from Terence R. McAuliffe, Chairman of Democratic National Committee, USA. (April 16, 2002).

**PERSONAL MEETINGS WITH DIGNITARIES:**

Honorable. Teng-Hui-Lee, President of Taiwan. 1999.
Hon. Leonard Fernandez, President of Dominican Republic. 1999.
Prince. Ahmed Fahad Al-Turki, (Saudi Arabia). 2000.
Benazir Bhutto, Prime Minister of Pakistan, 2001.
Dr. Keith Mitchell, Prime Minister of Grenada, West Indies. 2003-2004.

Pierre Charles, Prime Minister of Dominica, West Indies, 2003.

Mr. Charles Sovran, Foreign Minister of Dominica, 2003.

Robert H. O. Corbin Leader & Deputy-Prime-Minister (PNC) Guyana 2004.

Hon. P. J. Peterson, Prime Minister of Jamaica. 2004.

Dr. Kenny D. Anthony, Prime Minister of Saint Lucia, West Indies. 2005.

Hon. Owen Arthur, Prime Minister of Barbados, West Indies. 2005.

Michael de la Bastide, "Chief Justice" and President of the Caribbean Islands. 2005.

Mahmood M. Hussain, the Private Office of His Royal Highness. Dr. Sheikh-

Sultan Bin Khalifa Bin Zayed Al Nahyan, Abu-Dhabi, U.A.E. 2005.

Sultan S. Al Mansoori, Saeed & Mohammed Alnaboodah, Dubai, UAE 2005.

Ibrahim A. Gambari, Under-Secretary-General (United Nations) 2006.

Hon. Villasarao Deshmukh, Chief Minister of Maharashtra, India, 2006.

Hon. Ashok Chovan, Minister of Industries, Maharashtra, India, 2006.

Hon. Liu Bowie, Ambassador of China, United Nations, 2006.

Senator Einstein Louison, Ministry of Agriculture, Grenada.

Hon. Mark Isaac, Minister of State, Grenada, West Indies.

Hon. Brenda Hood, Minister for Tourism, Civil Aviation, Culture, Grenada.

Wayne Smith, Mayor, Township of Irvington, New Jersey, USA.

Orlando J. Moreno, Brigadier General & Military Advisor, (UNO) Venezuela.

As well as many more

# CONTENTS

# CHAPTER 1

## THE ENIGMATIC BOOKSTORE OWNER

Rachel Sullivan had always been captivated by the allure of antiquarian books and the whispers of history they held within their pages. Her love for the written word led her to open "Past Pages," a charming little bookstore nestled in the heart of New York City. The cozy shop exuded an old-world charm, with shelves lined with weathered novels and the aroma of aged paper wafting through the air.

Rachel was a woman of impeccable taste, her vibrant red hair framing her face as she busily arranged a display of vintage books on a worn wooden table. Her eyes sparkled with a blend of excitement and reverence as she carefully dusted off each tome, appreciating the stories they held within.

Her passion for the past ran deep, and she had a knack for unearthing forgotten treasures that would bring joy to her customers. Her bookstore became a haven for history buffs, bibliophiles, and those seeking solace in the enchantment of a bygone era.

It was on an ordinary day, the sun casting a warm glow through the small windows, that Rachel's life took an extraordinary turn. A peculiar package arrived at her doorstep, addressed to "Past Pages." She peered at the return address, but it bore no recognizable name or place. Intrigued, she carried the package inside and carefully opened it, revealing an array of classic novels, their spines well-worn with age.

As Rachel began to unpack the books, her fingers grazed something unexpected. Tucked within the pages of a particularly weathered leather-bound book, she discovered a collection of handwritten letters, their ink faded with time. Curiosity sparked within her as she realized that each letter was addressed to a 'Rachel' and signed by a certain 'James Thornton.'

Her heart skipped a beat as she read the first letter, its words filled with a profound sense of longing and love. James poured his heart onto the page, expressing a connection that transcended the boundaries of time. The letters were a testament to a love that defied logic and reason, an extraordinary romance woven through the fabric of forgotten time.

Rachel couldn't help but wonder who this mysterious James Thornton was and how these letters had found their way into her hands. Was it a mere coincidence, or was there a deeper purpose behind their arrival at her bookstore?

With trembling hands, she continued to read the letters, her emotions swirling like a tempestuous sea. James spoke of shared dreams, stolen glances across vast distances, and a love that burned brighter than the stars themselves. He mentioned events that hadn't yet occurred, weaving the future seamlessly into the past. It was as if James had a profound knowledge of the world, one that surpassed the limits of ordinary existence.

As Rachel delved deeper into the letters, the veil between reality and possibility began to blur. She found herself yearning for this enigmatic James Thornton, a man she had never met but who had somehow managed to touch her soul through the ink on those pages.

With a sense of determination, Rachel set out to unravel the mystery that had landed on her doorstep. She combed through her vast collection of books, searching for any clues or references to James Thornton. Hours turned into days as she tirelessly pursued every lead, her fascination growing with each passing moment.

The days melted away as Rachel's world became consumed by the letters and the tantalizing prospect of discovering the truth behind James Thornton. Her bookstore, once a haven for her customers, now became a playground for her quest for answers.

As she wove through the stacks of books, the scent of aged paper filling her senses, Rachel couldn't help but feel a magnetic pull towards James. It was as if he existed outside the boundaries of time, a romantic figure with whom she shared a connection that defied logic and explanation.

Little did she know that her journey would take her to places she had never imagined, and her heart would soon be caught in the throes of a love story that transcended the limitations of time itself?

With each passing day, Rachel's obsession with the letters grew stronger. She found herself unable to resist their magnetic pull, their words etching themselves into her heart. The more she read, the more she felt a profound connection to James Thornton, as if his soul was reaching out to hers from across the expanse of time.

The quaint bookstore, "Past Pages," became a sanctuary for Rachel as she delved further into the mystery. She spent countless hours surrounded by towering shelves of books, her fingertips tracing the spines, hoping to uncover a hidden clue or a forgotten reference that would shed light on James Thornton's existence.

Late into the night, as the city outside slumbered, Rachel would sit by a dimly lit lamp, the letters spread before her like a map to an unknown treasure. Each stroke of the pen seemed to whisper secrets of a love that transcended the boundaries of time. And in those quiet moments, Rachel could almost feel James' presence, his warmth enveloping her as she immersed herself in his words.

But as the days turned into weeks, doubt began to creep into Rachel's mind. Was this all an elaborate ruse? Could these letters simply be the product of an overactive imagination or a cruel prank? She questioned herself, the authenticity of the letters, and her own longing for a connection that may only exist within the realm of fiction.

Yet, no matter how hard she tried to dismiss the letters as mere fantasy, the synchronicity of the events described within them was too uncanny to ignore. Concerts at the Lincoln Center, a café opening on 5th Avenue, and even her favorite book being published - all were mentioned in James' letters before they became reality.

Rachel's rational mind battled with her burgeoning belief in something beyond comprehension. The enigmatic bookstore owner was torn between skepticism and an undeniable yearning for the truth. She couldn't shake the feeling that James Thornton and the letters held the key to a destiny she was destined to unravel.

Rachel stood at the precipice of a remarkable journey. The mysterious arrival of the leather book and the collection of letters had ignited a spark within her, fanning the flames of curiosity and enchantment. She had yet to fully understand the extent of the mysteries surrounding James Thornton, but one thing was certain - her life would never be the same.

With determination coursing through her veins, Rachel vowed to uncover the truth behind the letters and the enigmatic figure who had penned them. The journey ahead promised excitement, romance, and a profound exploration of love that surpassed the boundaries of time.

And so, with the turn of a page, Rachel Sullivan stepped further into the enigmatic world of "Past Pages," embarking on a quest that would intertwine her fate with that of James Thornton, and reveal the extraordinary power of a love that defied the constraints of forgotten time.

# CHAPTER 2

## THE DISCOVERY

Rachel Sullivan stood at the counter of her beloved bookstore, "Past Pages," carefully arranging a display of classic novels. The sunlight filtered through the small windows, casting a warm glow on the worn wooden table. The cozy ambiance of the shop embraced her as she took a moment to admire her labor of love.

As she arranged the last book, her gaze drifted to a nearby box, filled with a mix of novels from different eras. The box had arrived earlier in the day, a donation from a loyal customer who had recently inherited a collection of books. Rachel's curiosity was piqued as she wondered what hidden treasures might lie within its depths.

Setting aside her task, she walked over to the box and carefully lifted the lid. The scent of old paper wafted into the air, mingling with a hint of nostalgia. Her fingers brushed against the spines of the novels, feeling their history and the stories they held. As her hand moved deeper into the box, her fingers grazed something unexpected.

Nestled among the classic novels, Rachel's fingers encountered a book that stood out from the rest. Its worn leather cover bore the marks of time, and its edges were frayed, as if it had been cherished and handled countless times over the years. Curiosity sparked within her, and with a gentle tug, she freed the book from its confinement.

She cradled the weathered book in her hands, feeling its weight and the history it carried. There was an air of mystery surrounding it, as if it held secrets waiting to be unveiled. The title was barely discernible, faded by years of age and use. She ran her fingers over the embossed letters, trying to make out the words. "Whispers of Time," she whispered, her voice barely audible.

Intrigued by its aged appearance and the promise of forgotten tales, Rachel carried the book to a nearby table, bathed in the soft glow of a vintage lamp. With gentle reverence, she opened it, the pages crackling softly as they unfolded before her.

Within the book's weathered pages, Rachel discovered a collection of handwritten letters, neatly folded and carefully placed. The ink had faded with time, the elegant cursive writing a testament to the art of penmanship long forgotten. She picked up the first letter, its fragility apparent in her hands, and read the name on the envelope: 'Rachel.'

Her heart quickened with a mix of anticipation and trepidation. Was it mere coincidence that these letters shared her name? Or was it something more, a connection that transcended the boundaries of time itself? Eager to uncover the truth, Rachel unfolded the letter and began to read.

The words flowed across the page, each stroke of the pen imbued with a sense of longing and love. The author, James Thornton, poured his heart onto the page, expressing emotions that stirred something deep within Rachel's soul. It was as if the words were meant for her, as if James knew her intimately, even though they had never met.

James spoke of a connection that defied logic and reason, a bond forged in the depths of time. He described shared dreams, stolen glances across vast distances, and a love that burned brighter than the stars themselves. His words painted a vivid picture of a romance that surpassed the limitations of ordinary existence.

As Rachel delved deeper into the letters, she noticed something astonishing. James Thornton seemed to possess a profound knowledge of the world, referencing events that hadn't yet come to pass. A concert at the prestigious Lincoln Center, a small cafe opening on 5th Avenue, and even the publication of her favorite book were all mentioned in the letters, as if James possessed a glimpse into the future.

The enigmatic nature of the letters intrigued Rachel beyond measure. How could James Thornton have known about events that were yet to unfold? Was he a mere storyteller, or was there something more extraordinary at play? Her rational mind urged her to dismiss it as an elaborate hoax or a figment of her imagination. Yet, her intuition whispered that there was truth to be found within those pages.

Days turned into nights as Rachel delved further into the mystery of the letters. Her life revolved around the shop and the enigmatic presence of James Thornton. She found herself immersed in a world where time and reality blurred, where the past, present, and future danced in a cosmic embrace.

As she read each letter, Rachel began to decipher the hidden meanings and symbols within the words. There were subtle clues, hidden messages waiting to be unraveled. She meticulously studied the handwriting, searching for patterns and connections that could shed light on the enigma of James Thornton.

The bookstore, once bustling with customers, now became her sanctuary, a place where she could unravel the secrets that lay within the letters. She would sit for hours, surrounded by ancient tomes and the whispers of forgotten stories, piecing together the puzzle that was James Thornton and the love that spanned time.

Her friends and acquaintances noticed the change in Rachel. The fire in her eyes burned brighter, her spirit more alive than ever before. They couldn't help but be swept up in her excitement, drawn to the magnetic energy that emanated from her. They marveled at the way she spoke of the letters, of James Thornton, as if they were characters from a grand love story.

But as Rachel dove deeper into the letters, doubts gnawed at the corners of her mind. Was she becoming lost in a world of fantasy? Was she chasing shadows and ghosts, grasping at something that might not exist? She questioned her own sanity, wrestling with the conflict between reason and the pull of something greater than herself.

Yet, the synchronicity of events described in the letters was too uncanny to dismiss. Rachel found herself caught between skepticism and a deep yearning for the truth. She couldn't ignore the way her heart quickened at the mention of upcoming events that unfolded exactly as James had described.

With each passing day, Rachel's resolve grew stronger. She was determined to unravel the mystery, to uncover the truth that lay hidden within the letters. She combed through her vast collection of books, scouring through history and literature for any mention of James Thornton, for any clue that could guide her on her quest.

Her journey led her down countless paths, exploring forgotten tales and obscure references. She reached out to experts in various fields, seeking their insight and expertise. Slowly but surely, the puzzle pieces began to fit together, revealing a picture of a man who existed beyond the confines of time.

Rachel found herself on the precipice of discovery. The discovery of the leather-bound book and the collection of letters had opened a door to a world she never thought possible. She had yet to uncover the full extent of the mysteries surrounding James Thornton, but one thing was certain - her life had been forever changed.

With a mixture of trepidation and excitement, Rachel prepared to venture deeper into the enigmatic world that had found its way to her doorstep. The journey ahead promised not only the unveiling of a love story that defied the boundaries of time but also an exploration of her own identity and the power of belief.

As she closed the book, gently tucking the letters back into their rightful place within the leather-bound book, Rachel couldn't help but feel a sense of anticipation coursing through her veins. The discovery of the letters had ignited a flame within her, a flame that burned with an insatiable desire to uncover the truth behind James Thornton and the extraordinary connection they seemed to share.

As the chapter came to a close, Rachel Sullivan stood in the heart of "Past Pages," surrounded by the whispers of forgotten stories and the allure of time itself. Her fingers traced the spine of the weathered book, Whispers of Time, as she reflected on the journey that lay ahead.

With determination and an unyielding belief in the power of love, Rachel resolved to follow the breadcrumbs of history, chasing the echoes of James Thornton across the expanse of time. She knew that this path would not be without its challenges, but she was ready to embrace them, ready to unravel the mysteries that lay within the pages of the letters.

Her heart brimmed with anticipation as she imagined the stories yet to be discovered, the truths waiting to be unveiled. Rachel Sullivan, the enigmatic bookstore owner, had stepped onto a path that would lead her to a love that defied the constraints of time, to a destiny entwined with James Thornton.

Little did she know that the discovery of the leather book was only the beginning, a mere glimpse into the enchanting world that awaited her. With every word she read, with every step she took, Rachel would find herself drawn further into a romance that transcended the ordinary, a love story that spanned forgotten time.

As she locked the door of "Past Pages" behind her, the gentle sound of a turning key echoed through the empty shop. Rachel carried with her the weight of the leather-bound book and the anticipation of what lay ahead. The journey to uncover the truth and the path to James Thornton awaited her, beckoning her to venture into the depths of a love that would forever alter the course of her life.

And so, with a heart brimming with hope and a mind filled with curiosity, Rachel Sullivan embarked on a quest that would unravel the secrets of the letters, ignite a flame that defied the constraints of time, and lead her to the discovery of a love that whispered its echoes through the ages.

# CHAPTER 3

## THE HANDWRITTEN LETTERS

As Rachel Sullivan gingerly opened the pages of the weathered book, Whispers of Time, her heart fluttered with a mix of anticipation and curiosity. The journey she had embarked upon with the discovery of the letters had already woven an invisible thread between her and James Thornton, a connection that transcended time itself.

With each turn of the page, Rachel discovered a collection of handwritten letters tucked within the depths of the leather-bound book. They were neatly folded, their fragile edges bearing the marks of age. The ink had faded over time, but the emotions etched upon the paper were as vivid as ever.

Rachel's fingers trembled with a mix of excitement and trepidation as she picked up the first letter. Her name, 'Rachel,' was elegantly written on the envelope, and the signature below it read 'James Thornton.' She couldn't help but feel a profound sense of connection as she held the letter in her hands, as if it was meant solely for her.

With bated breath, she carefully unfolded the fragile paper, revealing a delicate dance of words that spoke of an undying love. James poured his heart onto the page, his emotions bleeding through every stroke of the pen. The depth of his affection resonated within Rachel, touching a part of her that had long yearned for a love that defied the boundaries of time.

The letters were a testament to a romance that spanned the ages, a love story interwoven with the fabric of forgotten time. As Rachel read through each letter, she marveled at James' eloquence and his ability to capture the essence of their connection, despite the chasm that separated them.

James spoke of a love that burned brighter than the stars, a love that surpassed the limitations of ordinary existence. His words whispered of stolen glances across vast distances, dreams shared in the twilight hours, and a bond that remained unbreakable throughout the passage of time.

But what astonished Rachel the most was the way James seemed to possess knowledge of events that were yet to happen. The letters contained references to moments and milestones that were still to unfold in Rachel's life. A concert at the prestigious Lincoln Center, a small café opening on 5th Avenue, and even the publication of her favorite book were all described with uncanny precision.

Each letter held its own intimate narrative, weaving together the present, the past, and the future. It was as if James Thornton was not only a witness to these moments but a participant, connected to Rachel in ways that transcended the ordinary bounds of human understanding.

As Rachel immersed herself in the letters, she discovered hidden depths within the pages. The handwriting held subtle nuances and hidden symbols, as if James had left breadcrumbs for her to follow, guiding her through the labyrinthine paths of their shared destiny.

Days turned into nights as Rachel poured over the letters, her mind consumed by the enigmatic figure of James Thornton. She found herself yearning for their connection to deepen, for their souls to intertwine in a dance that traversed time and space.

With each new letter, Rachel's heart opened wider, embracing the possibility of a love that defied the constraints of logic and reason. The letters became a lifeline, connecting her to James in ways she could never have imagined. Through the ink on those pages, she felt his presence, his essence seeping into her very being.

But amid the magic and wonder, doubts began to creep into Rachel's mind. Could this be a figment of her imagination? A whimsical dream that would vanish with the morning light? She wrestled with the conflicting forces of skepticism and the deep longing within her heart.

Yet, the synchronicity of the events described within the letters was too profound to dismiss as mere coincidence. The concert at the Lincoln Center had come to pass exactly as James had written. The small cafe opening on 5th Avenue was now a bustling hub of activity. And even the publication of her favorite book had occurred, leaving Rachel in awe of the power contained within those letters.

The more Rachel delved into the letters, the stronger her conviction grew. There was a deeper truth waiting to be unveiled, a hidden connection between her and James that defied all rational explanations. The evidence lay before her, etched in the ink of the handwritten words.

Driven by an insatiable curiosity, Rachel meticulously analyzed each letter, searching for hidden meanings and messages that lay beneath the surface. She began to notice recurring motifs, cryptic symbols, and even snippets of poetry woven within the prose. It was as if James was leaving breadcrumbs for her, a trail of clues to follow on their journey.

Late into the night, Rachel would sit in her cozy bookstore, bathed in the warm glow of a vintage lamp, surrounded by the whispers of the past. The letters spread before her, she would decipher the secrets hidden within their lines. With a mix of excitement and determination, she embarked on a quest to unlock the mysteries contained within the words of James Thornton.

Days turned into weeks, and Rachel's world became consumed by the letters. She barely noticed the passing of time as she charted the intricacies of their connection. Her customers, who had come to adore her bookstore, couldn't help but be captivated by the transformation they witnessed. They would catch glimpses of Rachel lost in thought, her eyes shining with an ethereal light, and they couldn't help but wonder about the extraordinary love that had captured her heart.

But Rachel's journey was not without its moments of doubt and hesitation. The logical part of her mind fought against the fantastical nature of the letters. How could she trust in something so intangible, so beyond the realms of her understanding? Yet, every time she attempted to dismiss them as figments of her imagination, she would encounter another moment of synchronicity, another event that unfolded precisely as James had described.

It was as if the letters themselves held a power, a connection to a higher realm, guiding Rachel along a predetermined path. And as much as she longed for tangible proof, Rachel had come to realize that the proof she sought would not be found in the physical realm. It would come from the depths of her own heart, from the unspoken truths that resonated within her soul.

The collection of letters became Rachel's source of inspiration, a wellspring of hope and wonder. They fueled her imagination and allowed her to dream of a love that transcended the limitations of time. Through the words of James Thornton, she began to envision a future that defied the boundaries of ordinary existence.

In the quiet moments of solitude, Rachel would close her eyes and imagine herself standing beside James, feeling the warmth of his presence, and sharing a love that knew no bounds. She would envision the events he had foretold, the milestones they would experience together, and the everlasting connection that would withstand the test of time.

The letters became her sanctuary, a portal into a world where love was not confined by the constraints of reality. They became a testament to the power of belief, reminding Rachel that sometimes, the greatest truths lie in the realm of the unseen.

Rachel Sullivan had become intimately acquainted with the handwritten letters of James Thornton. She had discovered an undying love that coursed through the pages, reaching out to her heart. The letters had become a mirror, reflecting the depths of her own desires, her longing for a love that defied the limitations of the world she knew.

With each passing day, Rachel's connection to James grew stronger. She could feel his presence in every word, his essence intertwining with her own. The letters had become more than just ink on paper—they were a lifeline, a tether that bound their souls together across the vast expanse of time.

But even as Rachel marveled at the depth of their connection, a part of her remained cautious. She understood the fragility of belief, the delicate balance between hope and skepticism. She knew that she needed more than just the letters to validate her feelings, to solidify the reality of their love.

And so, with a newfound determination, Rachel embarked on a mission to uncover the truth behind James Thornton. She meticulously researched historical records, scoured libraries and archives, searching for any mention of his name, any evidence of his existence beyond the realm of the letters.

Her search led her down countless paths, each one promising a glimmer of hope, only to fade into disappointment. Yet, Rachel refused to give up. She was driven by an unwavering faith in the connection she felt, a belief that their love was not confined to the pages of a book but extended into the very fabric of reality.

As Rachel dug deeper, she began to discover fragments of James Thornton's presence scattered throughout history. A mention in an old newspaper article, a faded photograph tucked away in an archive—each piece added another layer to the portrait of the man who had penned those heartfelt letters.

Through her research, Rachel uncovered the threads that connected James Thornton to significant events in the past. His name was associated with moments of cultural significance, his presence felt in the lives of influential figures. It became clear that James Thornton was no ordinary man; he was a figure woven into the tapestry of time itself.

The more Rachel uncovered, the more her belief solidified. James's knowledge of future events, his profound understanding of their connection—it all pointed to a reality that transcended the limitations of the physical world. It was a reality where time was fluid, where love could span centuries, and where the impossible became possible.

With each revelation, Rachel's heart swelled with a sense of awe and wonder. She realized that their love story was not confined to the boundaries of their individual lives but was part of a grander narrative, a story that had been unfolding through the ages. The letters were merely the vessels through which their love was expressed, but the essence of their connection went far beyond mere words on a page.

, Rachel stood at the precipice of a profound realization. She understood that the discovery of the letters was just the beginning of a journey that would test her beliefs and challenge her understanding of the world. It was a journey that would lead her to confront the very nature of reality and the power of love.

Armed with the knowledge she had uncovered and fueled by the depths of her love for James, Rachel was ready to take the next step. She was ready to embrace the mysteries that lay ahead and venture into the unknown, guided by the words of the letters and the unwavering belief in a love that defied all boundaries.

And so, with a heart filled with courage and a mind open to the infinite possibilities, Rachel Sullivan prepared to step further into the enigmatic world of James Thornton. The journey she had embarked upon was not just a search for answers; it was a voyage of self-discovery, a testament to the power of love and the enduring nature of human connection.

As she closed the book, gently tucking the letters back into their resting place, Rachel knew that the path she had chosen would lead her to a destiny intertwined with James Thornton. The chapters ahead promised adventure, revelation, and a love that would transcend the constraints of time itself. And with that knowledge, she set forth, ready to unravel the secrets of the handwritten letters

# CHAPTER 4

## CURIOSITY AWAKENS

As Rachel Sullivan delved deeper into the collection of handwritten letters, a whirlwind of emotions swept through her. The uncanny coincidences and references to events that hadn't yet happened left her in a state of both fascination and confusion. She couldn't help but contemplate the possibilities that lay before her—a world of time travel or a cleverly orchestrated hoax.

Sitting amidst the shelves of her cozy bookstore, "Past Pages," Rachel turned the letters over in her hands, her mind racing with thoughts and questions. How could James Thornton have known about these future events? Was it mere coincidence, or was there something more extraordinary at play? The rational part of her mind urged her to dismiss it as an elaborate fabrication, a cleverly constructed illusion. But her heart, drawn to the depth of emotion within the letters, whispered that there was truth to be found within those pages.

Rachel's love for antiquarian books and history had always fueled her imagination. She had often found solace in the stories that stretched the boundaries of time, tales of forgotten civilizations, and the enigmatic concept of time travel. But now, faced with the possibility of its reality, she was filled with a mixture of excitement and apprehension.

As she contemplated the idea of time travel, Rachel's thoughts spun like a whirlwind. She recalled the stories she had read, the theories proposed by scientists and philosophers alike. The idea that one could traverse through time, witness the grand tapestry of history, and even alter its course had always fascinated her. But to think that James Thornton, a man she had never met, might possess this power—it was both exhilarating and daunting.

However, the skeptic within Rachel couldn't be easily silenced. She considered the possibility of an intricate hoax, a meticulously crafted illusion designed to captivate her imagination and heart. The thought left a bitter taste in her mouth, casting a shadow over the emotions that had begun to bloom within her. She wondered if someone had gone through great lengths to play with her feelings, to deceive her into believing in something that was nothing more than fiction.

Days turned into nights as Rachel wrestled with her doubts and yearnings. The letters held a power over her, tugging at the strings of her heart, urging her to believe in something beyond the realm of the ordinary. But she couldn't dismiss the nagging voice in her mind—the voice of reason that reminded her of the dangers of falling into the trap of wishful thinking.

Seeking solace in her bookstore, Rachel turned to the shelves lined with books that had stood the test of time. She sought answers within their pages, searching for accounts of others who had grappled with the concept of time travel and extraordinary connections. The tales she encountered ranged from the whimsical to the philosophical, each offering its own interpretation of the enigmatic phenomenon.

She read about the concept of parallel universes and the intricate web of possibilities that existed beyond the realm of her perception. The idea that there could be multiple timelines, each unfolding with its own set of events, intrigued her. Perhaps James Thornton belonged to a different timeline—one in which their connection was not bound by the constraints of time.

As Rachel continued her exploration, she stumbled upon a book written by a renowned physicist who had delved into the realm of time travel. His words resonated with her, offering a glimmer of insight into the possibilities that lay before her. The physicist argued that time, as humans understood it, was a construct—a product of perception and consciousness. He postulated that if one could alter their perception, they could potentially navigate through time in a way that defied conventional understanding.

These newfound perspectives only fueled Rachel's curiosity further. She couldn't ignore the nagging feeling that the letters held a deeper truth, a truth that extended beyond the realm of her own comprehension. With each passing day, her skepticism waned, gradually giving way to a sense of wonder and possibility.

Rachel decided to explore the letters from a different angle. Instead of fixating on the question of whether they were real or a hoax, she shifted her focus to the emotions they evoked within her. The love and longing that emanated from James's words felt too genuine to be fabricated. The depth of his connection to her, the intricacy of the details he described—it all pointed towards something profound and extraordinary.

She began to see the letters as a conduit, a bridge between their souls that defied the boundaries of time. Whether they were a result of time travel or an elaborate fabrication, they had served as a catalyst for their connection, awakening emotions within Rachel that she had never experienced before.

In the stillness of her bookstore, Rachel closed her eyes and let her imagination wander. She envisioned a reality where time travel was possible, where love could span across the ages, and where James Thornton was a traveler navigating the currents of time to find her. It was a world of infinite possibilities, where the boundaries of the ordinary dissolved, and extraordinary connections could be forged.

With each passing moment, Rachel's curiosity blossomed like a flower in full bloom. She yearned to uncover the truth, to peel back the layers of mystery and delve deeper into the enigma of James Thornton. Her heart whispered that there was more to discover, a story waiting to unfold beyond the pages of the letters.

Driven by her newfound belief and fueled by her insatiable curiosity, Rachel embarked on a quest for answers. She reached out to experts in the fields of history, physics, and metaphysics, seeking their insights into the concept of time travel and the possibility of extraordinary connections.

Through her research, Rachel encountered a plethora of theories, ranging from the scientific to the metaphysical. Some proposed that time travel was feasible, given the manipulation of wormholes and the bending of space time. Others delved into the realm of consciousness, suggesting that the power of the mind could transcend the limitations of time and space.

As Rachel immersed herself in these theories, she found herself captivated by the notion that the letters could be a manifestation of a reality beyond her comprehension. The possibility of time travel ignited her imagination, expanding her worldview and freeing her from the constraints of her previous skepticism.

She began to envision a future where she and James could unite their perspectives, where their individual journeys through time could converge into a shared narrative. It was a future where their love would be the thread that bound them together, weaving through the fabric of time and defying the limitations of the ordinary.

Yet, amidst her newfound belief and excitement, Rachel remained cautious. She understood the importance of maintaining a balanced perspective, of considering the possibilities while remaining grounded in reality. She knew that her quest for answers would require patience, diligence, and an open mind.

Rachel found herself on the precipice of a profound transformation. Her journey into the enigma of James Thornton had awakened a curiosity within her that surpassed the boundaries of her previous understanding. She had contemplated the possibilities of time travel and the potential for an extraordinary connection, and her heart leaned towards embracing the belief in something greater than the ordinary.

Armed with her newfound perspective and fueled by her unwavering curiosity, Rachel Sullivan prepared to venture further into the depths of the mystery. The letters had become more than just ink on paper—they were a portal to a world where love and time intertwined, beckoning her to explore the uncharted territories of the extraordinary.

, Rachel knew that her journey was only beginning. The path ahead promised both answers and new questions, revelations and moments of uncertainty As Rachel Sullivan closed the chapter on her contemplation of time travel and extraordinary connections, she felt a renewed sense of purpose. The letters had stirred within her a profound curiosity, a thirst for knowledge that couldn't be quenched by mere speculation.

She resolved to approach her quest for answers with a scientific mindset. Rachel reached out to experts in the field of quantum physics, eager to delve into the mysteries of time and explore the potential for extraordinary connections. Conversations with renowned physicists and researchers expanded her understanding of the theoretical possibilities surrounding time travel.

One particular conversation left a lasting impression on Rachel. Dr. Amelia Westfield, a leading scientist in the field of temporal dynamics, shared her groundbreaking research on the manipulation of temporal vortices. Dr. Westfield hypothesized that certain individuals possessed a unique genetic predisposition that allowed them to interact with these vortices, enabling them to traverse through time.

The notion of genetic predisposition resonated deeply with Rachel. It provided a plausible explanation for James Thornton's ability to navigate the currents of time. If he possessed this genetic advantage, it would explain his uncanny knowledge of future events and their profound connection.

Inspired by Dr. Westfield's research, Rachel decided to undergo genetic testing herself. She wanted to understand if she carried the same genetic markers that could potentially enable her to access the realm of time travel. The results would offer a glimpse into her own potential and shed light on the enigma of her connection with James.

Days turned into weeks as Rachel awaited the results of the genetic testing. In the meantime, she continued her exploration of the letters, searching for hidden clues and deciphering the intricate symbolism within the words. The more she immersed herself in their world, the more convinced she became that there was a greater truth waiting to be unveiled.

Finally, the day arrived when Rachel received the long-awaited results. With a mix of anticipation and nervousness, she opened the envelope containing her genetic profile. The findings revealed a surprising revelation—she possessed the same genetic markers associated with individuals who had a heightened sensitivity to temporal vortices.

The discovery left Rachel in awe. It confirmed that there was something extraordinary about her connection with James Thornton, something that transcended the boundaries of the ordinary. The genetic evidence strengthened her belief in the reality of time travel and the possibilities that lay before her.

Armed with her genetic profile, Rachel sought out Dr. Westfield once more, eager to share her findings and seek guidance. Dr. Westfield was intrigued by Rachel's results and proposed a collaboration. Together, they would delve deeper into the mysteries of time travel, combining Rachel's unique genetic makeup with Dr. Westfield's groundbreaking research.

As Chapter 4 drew to a close, Rachel stood at the threshold of a new chapter in her journey. She had gone from skepticism to curiosity, from doubt to a growing belief in the extraordinary. The letters had become more than a mere curiosity—they had ignited a fire within her, propelling her towards a destiny she couldn't yet fully comprehend.

With the guidance of Dr. Westfield and armed with her genetic profile, Rachel was ready to push the boundaries of her understanding. She was determined to unlock the secrets of time travel and explore the depths of her connection with James Thornton. The path ahead was filled with unknowns, but Rachel embraced the uncertainty with a sense of wonder and anticipation, ready to step further into the enigmatic world that awaited her.

# CHAPTER 5

## JAMES THORNTON'S TIME-TRAVELING ADVENTURES

In the hidden corners of the universe, beyond the confines of ordinary time, a dashing figure known as James Thornton existed—a man whose very existence defied the boundaries of the present moment. James was a time traveler, a voyager through the currents of time, navigating the intricacies of history with a grace and elegance that seemed otherworldly.

His journey through time was not a choice but a destiny thrust upon him. Gifted with the ability to traverse the ages, James had come to understand the fragility of love in the realm of time travel. For every visit he made to Rachel, every stolen moment they shared, his very presence rewrote the tapestry of their destinies.

With each leap, James discovered new worlds and unearthed forgotten civilizations. He witnessed the rise and fall of empires, the birth of art and science, and the tender moments of human connection that transcended the barriers of time. And through it all, he carried with him a profound longing for the woman he had come to know through the ink-stained letters—Rachel Sullivan.

Their connection was unlike anything he had ever experienced. It defied the boundaries of time and space, reaching across the ages to intertwine their fates. From the moment he first discovered the power of their connection, James had embarked on a mission to protect Rachel, to guide her through the intricacies of their shared destiny.

In his travels, James had witnessed pivotal moments in Rachel's life, events that were yet to come to pass in her timeline. He had experienced the magic of their love, the longing that echoed through the corridors of time. And so, he began to leave behind the letters, carefully crafting them with the knowledge of their future encounters, hoping that Rachel would find them and follow the clues to their ultimate reunion.

As James journeyed through the annals of time, he discovered that the very act of time travel altered the fabric of existence. Each interaction with Rachel had consequences, rippling through the tapestry of time and leaving an indelible mark on their shared history. It was a delicate balance, a dance between the desire to be with her and the responsibility to protect the flow of time itself.

Yet, as James continued to witness the milestones of Rachel's life through the letters, his heart yearned for a connection that went beyond the written word. He longed to hold her in his arms, to feel the warmth of her presence, and to experience the love they had forged through the corridors of time. And so, he made a choice—a forbidden choice that would bring him closer to Rachel than ever before.

With a leap of faith, James decided to travel back to Rachel's timeline, to the present that she inhabited. It was a dangerous act, one that violated the laws of time travel, for the consequences of his actions could have far-reaching implications. But his love for

Rachel was stronger than any fear, and he was willing to risk everything for a chance at a future together.

As James arrived in Rachel's present, the anticipation surged through his veins. The world seemed to hold its breath, as if it, too, sensed the significance of their reunion. He knew that the last event mentioned in the letters, 'The Blooming of the Timeless Rose,' was drawing near. It was the culmination of their journey, the moment that held the promise of their love transcending the constraints of time.

Meanwhile, Rachel, driven by her unwavering belief in their connection, had been following the breadcrumbs left by James in the letters. Each event she experienced, each milestone she reached, brought her closer to the enigma that was James Thornton. Her heart beat with a mixture of excitement and trepidation as she approached the day of ' The Blooming of the Timeless Rose, a rare botanical event that held the key to their reunion.

The day arrived, bathed in the soft hues of twilight. The New York Botanical Garden hummed with anticipation; the air thick with the scent of blooming flowers. Rachel stood among the crowd, her heart pounding in her chest, her eyes scanning the faces, searching for the familiar warmth she had come to know through the letters.

And then, as if guided by an invisible force, their eyes met. James Thornton emerged from the crowd, his gaze locked onto Rachel's, the connection between them stronger than ever before. The world around them seemed to fade away, leaving only the two of them standing in a universe of their own.

"Rachel," James whispered, his voice filled with a depth of emotion that echoed through her very soul. "I've been waiting a long time to meet you."

Tears welled up in Rachel's eyes as she took a step forward, drawn to him by an irresistible force. In that moment, everything fell into place—the letters, the journey, the love that had defied the confines of time. It was a culmination of a connection forged through ink-stained pages, a love story that had transcended the boundaries of ordinary existence.

They stood before each other, no longer separated by the constraints of time travel. James reached out and took Rachel's hand, their fingers intertwining with a familiarity that felt as natural as breathing. It was a moment that defied explanation, a reunion that echoed through the ages.

As they embraced, a sense of completion washed over them. The journey that had brought them together, the trials and tribulations they had faced, all melted away in the embrace of their love. They had rewritten their destinies, defying the very laws of nature to be united.

In the days that followed, Rachel and James reveled in the joy of their newfound togetherness. They explored the depths of their connection, sharing stories of their individual journeys through time. James revealed the wonders he had witnessed, the sights and sounds that had captivated him throughout history.

Their love bloomed like the timeless rose that had brought them together, vibrant and resilient. They embraced each moment, cherishing the present while carrying the weight of their shared past. Their bond served as a reminder that love, when fueled by belief and an unwavering connection, could overcome any obstacle.

Together, Rachel and James continued their exploration of time and love. They embarked on their own time-traveling adventures, venturing into the past and future, their hearts intertwined as they created new memories that defied the constraints of time.

As the years unfolded, Rachel's quaint bookstore, "Past Pages," transformed into a sanctuary for those seeking stories that stretched the boundaries of time. The shop became a hub of wonder and discovery, a place where the echoes of forgotten love stories could be heard, and where the power of belief in the extraordinary was celebrated.

And through it all, the letters remained a cherished relic, a testament to a love that had transcended the limitations of forgotten time. They served as a reminder of the remarkable journey that Rachel and James had embarked upon, and of the power of a connection that defied the constraints of the ordinary.

In the end, The Letters of Forgotten Time was more than just a love story—it was a testament to the resilience of the human spirit, the enduring power of love, and the belief that extraordinary connections can be forged in the most unexpected of ways. It was a tale that left an indelible mark on those who encountered it, a story whispered through the ages, carrying with it the promise that love, when nurtured with unwavering belief, can transcend the boundaries of time itself.

# CHAPTER 6

## THE GROWING CONNECTION

As Rachel Sullivan immersed herself further into the collection of heartfelt letters from James Thornton, she found herself increasingly drawn to him. The connection they shared, forged through the ink-stained pages, grew stronger with each passing day. The letters became a lifeline, carrying their emotions and thoughts across the expanse of time, intertwining their souls in a tapestry of love and longing.

With a newfound determination, Rachel began to decipher the hidden meanings and clues woven within the correspondence. She studied the intricacies of James's words, searching for patterns, symbolism, and messages beyond the surface. The more she delved into the letters, the more she sensed that they held a deeper truth, a roadmap leading to the heart of their connection.

Late into the night, Rachel would sit in her quiet corner of the bookstore, surrounded by stacks of books and the echoes of forgotten stories. With a magnifying glass in hand, she meticulously examined each letter, scanning for subtle nuances and hidden messages that would shed light on the mysteries they held.

As she unraveled the layers of meaning within the letters, Rachel discovered a symphony of symbolism and clues. The recurring references to specific locations, dates, and events formed a delicate web that linked their past, present, and future. She deciphered the intricate metaphors and poetic language that James had employed, unraveling the hidden path that led to their ultimate reunion.

Guided by the letters, Rachel embarked on a series of adventures. She followed the breadcrumbs left by James, traversing the city streets, exploring historical landmarks, and immersing herself in the experiences he had described. Each step brought her closer to the essence of their connection, deepening her understanding of the love they shared.

With every new revelation, Rachel's heart swelled with a mixture of awe and tenderness. The letters not only captured the essence of their connection but also reflected James's profound knowledge of her thoughts, desires, and dreams. It was as if he possessed an intimate understanding of her very being, transcending the boundaries of time and space.

But as Rachel continued her exploration, she also encountered moments of doubt and uncertainty. The weight of the extraordinary connection they shared was a double-edged sword. While it filled her with a sense of wonder, it also tested the limits of her beliefs. She questioned the boundaries of possibility and grappled with the implications of a love that defied conventional understanding.

During these moments of introspection, Rachel sought solace in her conversations with Dr. Amelia Westfield. The esteemed scientist provided a rational perspective, grounding Rachel's explorations in the realm of scientific inquiry. Dr. Westfield acknowledged the enigmatic nature of their connection but encouraged Rachel to embrace the extraordinary and view it as a gateway to uncharted territories of understanding.

With Dr. Westfield's guidance and her own intuition as compasses, Rachel continued to decode the hidden meanings within the letters. She uncovered references to ancient texts, mystical symbols, and philosophical concepts that hinted at a deeper truth. The letters were not just declarations of love but also gateways to knowledge, invitations to explore the realms of history, philosophy, and the human experience.

As Rachel immersed herself in this intellectual and emotional journey, she discovered that the letters were not just a means of communication but also a vessel for James's wisdom and insights. Through his words, she gained a profound understanding of the world, of the ebb and flow of time, and the beauty found in the transient nature of existence.

With each revelation, Rachel's love for James grew deeper. His vulnerability, his unwavering affection, and the depth of his understanding left an indelible mark on her heart. It was not just the connection forged through the letters but the resonance of their souls that bound them together.

in a way that defied conventional explanation. Their love was not just rooted in the present moment but transcended the limitations of time itself.

As Rachel's understanding of the hidden meanings within the letters grew, so too did her appreciation for the power of their connection. She realized that their love story was not confined to the physical realm, but spanned across the vast expanse of time, echoing through the ages. It was a love that had endured, even when they were separated by the constraints of different timelines.

The letters became a source of solace and inspiration for Rachel. In moments of doubt, she would retreat to the quiet corners of her bookstore, immersing herself in the heartfelt words that James had penned. His vulnerability, expressed through the ink on the pages, mirrored her own, and she found comfort in the shared experience of longing and yearning.

With each passing day, Rachel's admiration for James's wisdom and insight deepened. His knowledge of history, art, and the intricacies of the human experience permeated the letters, enriching her understanding of the world. Through his eyes, she saw history unfold in new and profound ways, witnessing the beauty and tragedy of the past with a newfound appreciation.

The hidden meanings within the letters guided Rachel to places she had never been, introduced her to people she had never met, and expanded her horizons in unimaginable ways. She found herself exploring ancient libraries, wandering through forgotten ruins, and engaging in conversations with scholars and thinkers who had shaped the course of history. Through these experiences, she felt a deep connection not only to James but also to the tapestry of human existence.

As Rachel delved deeper into the labyrinth of hidden clues, she began to sense that their connection was not limited to the confines of the letters. It extended beyond the pages, weaving through the fabric of her own life. She started noticing synchronicities—moments of serendipity and alignment with the events James had described. It was as if their connection had transcended the realm of words and manifested itself in the tangible world around her.

These synchronicities served as reminders of the profound bond they shared—a bond that defied rational explanation. Rachel's skepticism waned as she witnessed the events unfold exactly as

James had foretold. The precise details he had described in the letters became a testament to the authenticity of their connection.

But even as Rachel embraced the extraordinary nature of their love, she couldn't help but question the implications of their connection. What did it mean for their individual lives, their identities, and the choices they would make? The weight of the unknown loomed over her, challenging her to reconcile the extraordinary with the practical realities of existence.

However, amidst the questions and uncertainties, Rachel knew one thing for certain—she was irrevocably drawn to James Thornton. His words, his vulnerability, and the connection they shared had opened her heart to a love she had never imagined possible. And she was willing to embrace the mysteries and uncertainties that came with it, for their love was an affirmation that life was not bound by the constraints of the ordinary.

Rachel Sullivan stood at a crossroads—her belief in the extraordinary solidified, her connection with James growing deeper with each passing moment. The hidden meanings and clues within the letters had brought them closer, intertwining their destinies in a tapestry of love and discovery.

With an unwavering faith in their connection, Rachel prepared to embark on the next phase of their journey. The letters had become a roadmap leading her to a future intertwined with James, where time and love transcended the boundaries of the ordinary. It was a journey filled with uncertainties, but she was driven by a profound sense of purpose and a belief that their love was worth the risks and challenges they may face along the way.

As Rachel delved further into the hidden meanings and clues within the letters, she also discovered a newfound strength within herself. The love and connection she shared with James empowered her to embrace the unknown, to step into uncharted territories with courage and determination.

She became bolder in her pursuit of understanding, seeking out experts, and engaging with individuals who had explored the mysteries of time and connection. Conversations with philosophers, historians, and spiritual guides expanded her perspective, offering diverse insights into the nature of love and the possibilities that lie beyond conventional understanding.

Rachel's exploration also led her to engage with individuals who claimed to have experienced their own encounters with extraordinary connections. Their stories affirmed her belief in the power of love and the existence of realms beyond the visible. Through these interactions, she gained a network of support—a community of individuals who shared a common thread of embracing the extraordinary.

With each step forward, Rachel's connection with James intensified. The letters had served as a bridge, allowing their souls to intertwine across the fabric of time. Through their shared experiences, she developed a profound understanding of James's essence—an understanding that transcended physical appearances and encompassed the depths of his being.

She could sense his presence even in his absence, his energy resonating within her like a gentle hum. Their connection had become a source of strength, a guiding force that propelled her forward. In moments of doubt, she would close her eyes and feel his presence, drawing comfort and reassurance from the unbreakable bond they shared.

The more Rachel deciphered the hidden meanings within the letters, the more she realized that their connection went beyond the confines of their individual lives. It was part of a grand tapestry—a tapestry woven by the collective experiences of humanity. Their love story was a reflection of the human quest for connection and transcendence, echoing the timeless yearning for something greater than oneself.

Rachel's perception of reality shifted, embracing a broader understanding of existence. She began to see the interconnectedness of all things, the intricate threads that bound every individual to the grand design of the universe. The letters had become a symbol of this interconnectivity—a testament to the power of love and the eternal dance of souls across time and space.

Rachel stood on the precipice of a profound transformation. The hidden meanings and clues within the letters had not only deepened her connection with James but also expanded her understanding of the nature of love and the possibilities that lay before them.

With a heart filled with determination and a mind open to the extraordinary, Rachel Sullivan prepared to embrace the next phase of their journey. She was ready to step into the unknown, to unravel the remaining mysteries, and to forge a future that defied the limitations of time and space.

The growing connection between Rachel and James had become an unstoppable force—an interplay of hearts, minds, and souls that defied conventional boundaries. They were on the cusp of something extraordinary, a love story that would leave an indelible mark on the tapestry of time.

As they prepared to embark on their shared destiny, Rachel's faith in their connection remained unwavering. Guided by the hidden meanings and clues within the letters, they would navigate the complexities of time and explore the depths of their love. Together, they would transcend the ordinary and embrace a reality where their hearts could unite, forever bound by the power of an extraordinary connection.

# CHAPTER 7

## JAMES' FORBIDDEN LOVE

Within the depths of James Thornton's being, a tumultuous battle raged—a battle between his heart's desire and the unforgiving laws of time. He had fallen irrevocably in love with Rachel Sullivan, a woman who existed in a different timeline. Their connection transcended the ordinary, defying the boundaries that governed the lives of mere mortals. But for James, a time traveler burdened with the weight of forbidden love, the consequences loomed ominously.

As James journeyed through time, he witnessed the beauty and tragedy of the world. He explored distant civilizations, observed pivotal historical events, and delved into the depths of human existence. But with every stolen moment he spent with Rachel, his timeline began to unravel, threatening to erase his very existence.

The realization of the consequences weighed heavily on James's soul. Love, a luxury that time travelers could ill afford, became both his salvation and his downfall. The more he intertwined his life with Rachel's, the more he risked erasing his own existence from the fabric of time. It was a precarious dance on the edge of a knife, each step carrying the weight of irrevocable change.

James yearned for a future where he and Rachel could be together, where their love would transcend the barriers of time and space. He dreamed of a reality where he could rewrite his own timeline, altering the course of history to ensure their eternal connection. But the laws of time were unforgiving, reminding him of the delicate balance that held the universe together.

Every interaction, every moment shared with Rachel, had a ripple effect—an impact that reverberated throughout the timeline, altering the lives of countless individuals. James understood the gravity of his actions, the potential devastation that could unfold if he defied the laws of nature. He wrestled with the knowledge that his love for Rachel could rewrite the history of the world, forever altering the course of human existence.

In the quiet solitude of his travels, James grappled with his own identity. He questioned the morality of tampering with time, of bending the rules to satisfy his own desires. He yearned for a solution, a way to be with Rachel without compromising the delicate tapestry of the universe.

As he sought guidance from mentors and explored the ancient texts of time travel, James discovered the existence of an ancient artifact—a relic said to possess the power to navigate through time without disrupting the delicate balance of cause and effect. It was a glimmer of hope, a lifeline that offered the possibility of reconciling his love for Rachel with the sanctity of time itself.

Driven by a desperation fueled by love, James embarked on a treacherous journey to acquire the artifact. He navigated perilous terrains, outwitted formidable adversaries, and confronted his own fears and doubts. The quest tested his resolve, his unwavering belief in the power of love to defy even the most entrenched laws of nature.

As James drew closer to obtaining the artifact, he encountered ancient guardians—guardians of wisdom and guardians of time. They challenged his intentions, testing the purity of his love for Rachel. They warned him of the dangers that awaited, the consequences that would befall him if he dared to rewrite his own timeline.

With each trial, James's commitment to his love for Rachel grew stronger. He understood the risks, the potential cost of altering his own existence, but his heart refused to relinquish the hope of a future with her. He pressed on, determined to overcome every obstacle in his path.

When James finally obtained the artifact, he felt a surge of both trepidation and excitement. Holding it in his hands, he could feel the power coursing through his veins—the power to navigate through time, to rewrite his own destiny.

As James held the artifact in his hands, he couldn't help but marvel at its intricate design and the weight of responsibility it carried. With cautious anticipation, he harnessed its power, knowing that the fate of his love and the delicate balance of time hung in the balance.

With each step he took, James navigated the intricate threads of time, guided by the whispers of the artifact and fueled by his unwavering love for Rachel. He journeyed through the corridors of history, observing pivotal moments and rewriting the narrative of his own existence.

But with each alteration, James felt the tugging weight of consequences. The timeline trembled, threatening to unravel under the strain of his actions. He witnessed the collateral damage caused by his interventions—individuals whose lives were forever changed, events that unfolded in unexpected ways.

The price of love, it seemed, was a labyrinth of unforeseen repercussions.

Yet, despite the challenges and the mounting risks, James persevered. He had committed his heart and soul to Rachel, and he refused to let the constraints of time extinguish their love. With every alteration, he held onto the hope that their shared future would be one of happiness and fulfillment, even if it meant rewriting the very fabric of existence.

As the journey through time progressed, James encountered resistance from forces that sought to maintain the integrity of the timeline. Temporal guardians, ancient beings tasked with preserving the harmony of the universe, confronted him with questions of ethics and the consequences of his actions.

These guardians challenged James to consider the far-reaching implications of his love, urging him to examine the moral implications of altering the course of history for personal gain. They reminded him that tampering with time was a delicate dance, one that could have far-reaching consequences for the lives of countless individuals.

But James remained steadfast in his conviction. He acknowledged the weight of his choices, the sacrifices that would need to be made, but he couldn't deny the depth of his love for Rachel. The connection they shared was worth every risk, every sacrifice.

As James approached the climax of his journey, he stood at the precipice of rewriting his own timeline. The artifact pulsed with a mesmerizing energy, reflecting his hopes and fears. It represented a turning point—the moment when he would either forge a new path with Rachel or relinquish the dreams that had driven him throughout time.

With a mixture of trepidation and determination, James made his choice. He reached out to touch the fabric of time, embracing the unknown with open arms. The artifact hummed with power, guiding his hand as he rewrote the narrative of his own existence.

The consequences unfolded with an intensity that shook James to his core. The delicate balance of time shifted, and the ripples of his actions cascaded through history. The world transformed, and he watched as the pieces of his rewritten timeline fell into place, uncertain of what awaited him on the other side.

But amidst the uncertainty, James clung to the belief that his love for Rachel would endure. He trusted in the strength of their connection, the unyielding force that had propelled him through time itself. He held onto the hope that their love would withstand the challenges they faced, even as they walked a path that defied the boundaries of the ordinary.

James Thornton stood on the precipice of a new reality. The consequences of his actions loomed, but his heart beat with an unwavering faith in his love for Rachel. The forbidden love they shared had propelled him to rewrite his own timeline, defying the laws of nature in a desperate bid to be together.

# CHAPTER 8

## FOLLOWING THE CLUES

With new found determination, Rachel Sullivan embarked on a journey to unravel the hidden truths and follow the clues that had been carefully laid out within the letters. Each word, each line held a breadcrumb that led her closer to the enigma that was James Thornton. As she delved deeper into the intricate tapestry of the letters, she found herself immersed in a world of mystery and possibility.

Armed with her knowledge of the letters and the hidden meanings she had deciphered, Rachel set out to explore the events and locations that had been referenced within the correspondence. She became a detective, piecing together the fragments of James's world and following the trail he had left behind.

The first clue led Rachel to the majestic Lincoln Center, where a concert of breathtaking orchestral music was set to take place. She stood amidst the bustling crowd, her heart pounding with anticipation as the symphony filled the air. As the performance reached its crescendo, Rachel closed her eyes, allowing the music to transport her to a realm where time was but an ethereal concept.

In that moment, a stranger approached her, a twinkle in his eyes that mirrored the description James had penned. The encounter was brief but potent, leaving Rachel with a lingering sense of connection. It was as if the threads of their lives had briefly intertwined, leaving an indelible mark on both their souls.

Buoyed by the success of her first clue, Rachel continued her quest, each event unfolding like a chapter in a storybook. A small café on 5th Avenue, its aroma of freshly brewed coffee mingling with the scent of anticipation, became her next destination. As she sipped her latte, she marveled at the serendipity of the moment—the exact cafe that James had described in his letters, its ambiance a testament to their shared journey.

The clues led Rachel to museums, art galleries, and historical sites, each unveiling a fragment of the story. She found herself immersed in the beauty of a painting that mirrored a scene described in the letters, or standing before a statue that had been referenced in James's words. It was as if the universe itself conspired to bring them closer, guiding Rachel's steps as she unraveled the mystery.

As Rachel followed the breadcrumbs, she couldn't help but feel a growing connection to James with each passing event. The details he had penned in the letters were no longer mere words on paper—they had taken on a life of their own, woven into the fabric of her reality. The love they shared transcended time, echoing through the events that unfolded before her.

But amidst the excitement and wonder, Rachel also encountered moments of doubt. The magnitude of the journey she was undertaking weighed on her shoulders, and she questioned whether she was following a fool's errand—a mere figment of her imagination. The voice of skepticism whispered in her ear, challenging the reality of their connection and the significance of the clues she had discovered.

In these moments, Rachel sought solace in the memories of their encounters—the fleeting moments when their paths had crossed, even if only briefly. She would close her eyes, allowing the sensations to flood her senses—the warmth of a smile, the brush of a hand, the resonance of a shared moment. These memories anchored her, reminding her that the connection she felt with James was real and undeniable.

With each clue she followed, Rachel's understanding of James deepened. The events, the locations, and the references in the letters painted a portrait of a man who had traversed the tapestry of time with purpose and determination. She saw glimpses of his struggles, his yearning, and his unwavering love for her. The letters became a window into his soul, revealing a vulnerability that both captivated and humbled her.

As Rachel continued her journey, the clues led her to unexpected places. She found herself walking along the cobblestone streets of a historic neighborhood, guided by the faint echoes of laughter and music. It was there, in a quaint bookstore tucked away from the bustling city, that Rachel discovered a copy of her all-time favorite book, freshly published, just as James had foretold in one of his letters. Holding the book in her hands, she felt a surge of emotion—an affirmation that their connection extended beyond the boundaries of time.

With each event she uncovered, Rachel's determination grew, fueling her quest to uncover the truth about James. She tirelessly pursued every lead, following the trails of clues that seemed to be intricately designed to bring them closer. Each step she took, each mystery she unraveled, strengthened the bond between her and James, weaving their lives together in an extraordinary tapestry of love.

But as Rachel got closer to the truth, she also became aware of the complexities and sacrifices that accompanied their connection. She realized that the path they were on was not without its challenges. James had rewritten his own timeline, altering the course of history to be with her, and the consequences of his actions weighed heavily on his shoulders.

Rachel grappled with the knowledge that their love had come at a great cost—not only to James but potentially to the very fabric of time itself. She questioned whether the happiness they sought was worth the potential ramifications of their actions. Doubts and fears crept into her mind, threatening to overshadow the beauty of their connection.

In moments of uncertainty, Rachel found solace in the letters. She returned to them, reading and rereading the words that had forged their bond. They reminded her of the depth of James's love and his unwavering commitment to their shared destiny. The letters became her anchor, grounding her in the certainty of their connection, and giving her the strength to face the challenges ahead.

As Rachel approached the final clue, she could feel the weight of anticipation hanging in the air. The culmination of their journey, the moment they had both yearned for, was drawing near. She stood before the gates of the New York Botanical Garden, where the rare botanical event, "The Blooming of the Timeless Rose," was set to take place—a revelation she had discovered within the letters.

With bated breath, Rachel entered the garden, her heart pounding with a mixture of excitement and trepidation. The air was heavy with the scent of flowers, their vibrant colors painting a breathtaking landscape. She followed a path that wound through the garden, guided by the echoes of her footsteps and the whispers of her heart.

And then, amidst the crowd, she saw him—James Thornton, the man who had captured her heart through the ink-stained pages of the letters. His eyes, filled with a profound love and longing, met hers, and time stood still. In that moment, the world faded into the background, and all that mattered was the connection they shared—a love that transcended the boundaries of time and space.

"Rachel," James said, his voice filled with a mixture of awe and tenderness. "I've been waiting a long time to meet you."

Tears welled up in Rachel's eyes as she stepped forward, closing the distance between them. In that embrace, they found solace and completeness—a confirmation that their love was real, enduring, and worth every challenge they had faced.

Their journey, filled with clues and revelations, had led them to this pivotal moment. The events, the connections, and the trials they had endured had brought them together against all odds. Their love had triumphed over the constraints of time, defying the limitations that governed ordinary lives.

Found themselves entwined in an embrace that transcended the boundaries of time. In that moment, the world around them faded into insignificance, and they were immersed in the pure essence of their love.

Amidst the blooming roses and the enchanting ambiance of the garden, Rachel and James whispered words of devotion, their voices carrying the weight of a journey that had traversed the ages. The fragility and resilience of their connection had been tested, but it had withstood the trials and emerged stronger than ever.

As they stood amidst the beauty of the Timeless Rose, their love unfolded like the petals of a flower, unfurling with grace and delicacy. They reveled in the profound understanding that their connection was not bound by the limitations of time, but rather fueled by a love that defied the very fabric of reality.

In that sacred space, Rachel and James made a silent vow to cherish every moment they had together. They understood that their love, though extraordinary, required nurturing and care. They were willing to embrace the uncertainties that lay ahead, knowing that their bond was a testament to the infinite possibilities of the human heart.

With the sun setting on the horizon, casting a warm glow upon their intertwined hands, Rachel and James ventured forth into the uncharted territory of their shared future. They were determined to navigate the complexities of their love, armed with the knowledge that they held the power to rewrite their own destiny.

Marked the turning point in their journey—a juncture where they had unearthed the truth, followed the clues, and embraced the depths of their connection. Their love story, born from the pages of handwritten letters, had blossomed into a tale of resilience, courage, and the triumph of love over the constraints of time.

As the petals of the Timeless Rose continued to unfurl, Rachel and James knew that their journey was far from over. They had only just scratched the surface of the mysteries that lay before them, but they faced the unknown with a sense of exhilaration and an unyielding belief in the power of their love.

Rachel and James would navigate the intricacies of their intertwined destinies, defying the boundaries of time, and unearthing the secrets that had yet to be revealed. Together, they would embrace the extraordinary, surrendering to the profound connection that had brought them together and propelled them into a world where love reigned supreme.

As the night sky enveloped them, Rachel and James stood hand in hand, ready to embark on the next phase of their extraordinary journey—a journey that would test their resilience, challenge their perceptions, and illuminate the boundless possibilities of a love that transcended the constraints of time itself.

# CHAPTER 9

## THE INTERTWINED DESTINIES

In the aftermath of their encounter amidst the Timeless Rose, Rachel and James found themselves immersed in a world where their destinies were irrevocably intertwined. Their love, forged through the trials of time, had deepened into an unbreakable bond that defied the limitations of the ordinary.

As they embarked on the next phase of their journey, Rachel and James marveled at the depth of their emotional connection. They discovered a shared language, a silent communication that transcended words. With a single glance, a touch, or a gentle embrace, they could convey a universe of emotions—love, understanding, and unwavering support.

They reveled in the richness of their conversations, delving into the intricacies of life, love, and the meaning of existence. Their minds danced together, exploring the depths of knowledge and philosophy, each thought echoing and amplifying the other. In their togetherness, they found solace and a profound sense of belonging.

As they spent more time together, Rachel and James discovered the unique tapestry that had woven their lives together through the fabric of time. They unraveled the threads of coincidence and synchronicity that had brought them to this moment, recognizing the intricate design that had guided their paths. They marveled at the significance of their encounters, the serendipitous events that had shaped their individual stories, and ultimately converged to unite them in a love that defied the constraints of time.

Through shared experiences, they unearthed the profound impact they had on each other's lives. James, with his wisdom and experiences from different eras, offered Rachel a new perspective on the world. He challenged her beliefs, broadened her horizons, and awakened her to the infinite possibilities that lay within her grasp.

Rachel, in turn, ignited a flame within James—a flame that had been dampened by the burdens of time travel. Her unwavering love and unwavering belief in their connection reminded him of the beauty and joy that existed beyond the constraints of his temporal existence. With her by his side, he felt a renewed sense of purpose, a deep desire to embrace life and seize every precious moment they shared.

Together, Rachel and James embarked on a quest to uncover the secrets that lay hidden within the tapestry of time. They sought out ancient texts, consulted wise sages, and immersed themselves in the mystical realms of knowledge that had eluded them before. With each discovery, they pieced together fragments of a grand design—an interconnected web of lives, experiences, and destinies that had led them to this point.

As they delved deeper into the mysteries of time, Rachel and James encountered resistance—forces that sought to maintain the natural order of the universe. They faced challenges that tested their resolve, obstacles that threatened to tear them apart. But their love remained steadfast, a guiding light that propelled them forward even in the face of adversity.

They discovered that their intertwined destinies were not confined to their own love story. They became aware of the ripple effects their actions had on the lives of others, the individuals who had unknowingly played a part in their journey. Rachel and James realized that their love had the power to touch the lives of those around them, to inspire hope, and to rewrite the narratives of others.

With this newfound understanding, Rachel and James embraced their role as catalysts of change. They dedicated themselves to spreading love and compassion, using their unique connection to bring joy and healing to those they encountered. Their shared journey became a testament to the transformative power of love—a force that transcended the boundaries of time and left an indelible mark on the lives it touched, Rachel and James stood on the precipice of a future

In the aftermath of their encounter amidst the Timeless Rose, Rachel and James found themselves immersed in a world where their destinies were irrevocably intertwined. Their love, forged through the trials of time, had deepened into an unbreakable bond that defied the limitations of the ordinary.

As they embarked on the next phase of their journey, Rachel and James marveled at the depth of their emotional connection. They discovered a shared language, a silent communication that transcended words. With a single glance, a touch, or a gentle embrace, they could convey a universe of emotions—love, understanding, and unwavering support.

They reveled in the richness of their conversations, delving into the intricacies of life, love, and the meaning of existence. Their minds danced together, exploring the depths of knowledge and philosophy, each thought echoing and amplifying the other. In their togetherness, they found solace and a profound sense of belonging.

As they spent more time together, Rachel and James discovered the unique tapestry that had woven their lives together through the fabric of time. They unraveled the threads of coincidence and synchronicity that had brought them to this moment, recognizing the intricate design that had guided their paths. They marveled at the significance of their encounters, the serendipitous events that had shaped their individual stories, and ultimately converged to unite them in a love that defied the constraints of time.

Through shared experiences, they unearthed the profound impact they had on each other's lives. James, with his wisdom and experiences from different eras, offered Rachel a new perspective on the world. He challenged her beliefs, broadened her horizons, and awakened her to the infinite possibilities that lay within her grasp.

Rachel, in turn, ignited a flame within James—a flame that had been dampened by the burdens of time travel. Her unwavering love and unwavering belief in their connection reminded him of the beauty and joy that existed beyond the constraints of his temporal existence. With her by his side, he felt a renewed sense of purpose, a deep desire to embrace life and seize every precious moment they shared.

Together, Rachel and James embarked on a quest to uncover the secrets that lay hidden within the tapestry of time. They sought out ancient texts, consulted wise sages, and immersed themselves in the mystical realms of knowledge that had eluded them before. With each discovery, they pieced together fragments of a grand design—an interconnected web of lives, experiences, and destinies that had led them to this point.

As they delved deeper into the mysteries of time, Rachel and James encountered resistance—forces that sought to maintain the natural order of the universe. They faced challenges that tested their resolve, obstacles that threatened to tear them apart. But their love remained steadfast, a guiding light that propelled them forward even in the face of adversity.

They discovered that their intertwined destinies were not confined to their own love story. They became aware of the ripple effects their actions had on the lives of others, the individuals who had unknowingly played a part in their journey. Rachel and James realized that their love had the power to touch the lives of those around them, to inspire hope, and to rewrite the narratives of others.

With this newfound understanding, Rachel and James embraced their role as catalysts of change. They dedicated themselves to spreading love and compassion, using their unique connection to bring joy and healing to those they encountered. Their shared journey became a testament to the transformative power of love—a force that transcended the boundaries of time and left an indelible mark on the lives it touched.

Rachel and James stood on the precipice of a future that held infinite possibilities. They had come to realize that their intertwined destinies were not a coincidence, but a purposeful alignment of the universe—an intricate tapestry woven by love, time, and the forces that guided their paths.

With every step they had taken, every challenge they had faced, Rachel and James had grown stronger individually and as a couple. They had witnessed the transformative power of their connection, not only within their own lives but also in the lives of those they had touched along their journey. Their love had become a beacon of hope and inspiration, radiating its light into the darkest corners of the world.

As they looked toward the horizon, Rachel and James knew that their journey was far from over. The mysteries of time still beckoned, offering new discoveries and revelations. They were prepared to face whatever lay ahead, armed with the profound love that had carried them through the depths of time itself.

Their love had become a force that defied the limitations of the ordinary, transcending the boundaries of time and space. It was a love that had endured trials and tribulations, a love that had rewritten their destinies and reshaped the very fabric of their existence.

In the chapters that lay ahead, Rachel and James would continue to navigate the intricacies of their intertwined lives. They would explore the depths of their connection, unravel the secrets of time, and forge a path that defied convention. Their love story, etched in the annals of forgotten time, would continue to unfold, leaving an indelible mark on the hearts of all who encountered it.

As they stood together, ready to embark on the next phase of their extraordinary journey, Rachel and James shared a knowing smile. Their love had transcended the boundaries of time, defying the constraints of the ordinary. It was a love that had conquered the challenges of the past and had the power to shape the destiny of their future.

And so, hand in hand, Rachel and James embraced their intertwined destinies. With hearts filled with love, determination, and an unwavering belief in the extraordinary power of their connection, they stepped forward into the unknown. The mysteries of time awaited them, ready to reveal their secrets and unfold the chapters yet to be written.

Together, Rachel and James would continue their extraordinary love story, leaving an indelible mark on the tapestry of time itself.

-

# CHAPTER 10

## JAMES' FINAL LEAP

Is Rachel and James stood on the precipice of their intertwined destinies, they knew that the path ahead was filled with uncertainties and risks. The love they shared had defied the boundaries of time, but it also came with a heavy price—one that James was willing to pay.

In a daring move, James made the decision to take a forbidden leap back to Rachel's present time. It was a leap that defied the laws of nature, a leap that could potentially unravel the delicate threads of time and rewrite their shared history. But for James, the risks were worth it. He couldn't bear the thought of being separated from Rachel any longer.

With a mix of trepidation and determination, James harnessed the power of time travel once again. He delved into the depths of ancient knowledge, seeking the guidance and strength to undertake this perilous journey. The sages and mentors he encountered warned him of the dangers, the potential consequences that awaited him. They cautioned him about the fragility of time, reminding him that tampering with its delicate balance could have unforeseen repercussions.

But James had made up his mind. He was ready to confront the risks head-on, driven by an unwavering love that burned within his soul. He understood the sacrifices he would have to make—the potential erasure of his own existence, the rewriting of his own timeline. Yet, in his heart, he knew that being with Rachel was worth every perilous step.

As he prepared for the leap, James couldn't help but feel a mix of excitement and fear. The very fabric of time seemed to quiver with anticipation, sensing the disruption that his actions could cause. The weight of responsibility pressed upon him, but he drew strength from the love he shared with Rachel—a love that had defied the limitations of time itself.

With a final farewell to the world he had known, James took the leap. Time twisted and turned around him as he traversed the temporal currents, hurtling through the dimensions that separated him from Rachel's present. The journey was fraught with challenges and obstacles, but fueled by his unwavering love, he pressed on.

As James arrived in Rachel's present, he found himself in a world that felt simultaneously familiar and alien. He observed the changes that time had wrought—the subtle shifts in technology, the evolving landscape of the city, and the passage of years etched upon the faces of those around him. It was a world that he had only glimpsed through the words of the letters, and now he stood amidst it, ready to embrace the reality he had yearned for.

But the risks of his forbidden leap remained ever-present. James knew that the timeline had been altered, and the consequences of his actions were uncertain. He had rewritten his own existence, defying the laws that governed the natural flow of time. The delicate balance hung in the balance, and the potential for chaos loomed.

Yet, in the midst of uncertainty, James was driven by a singular purpose—to find Rachel, to hold her in his arms, and to continue their extraordinary love story. He embarked on a quest to locate her, following the threads of their intertwined destinies that still pulsed within his heart.

As he navigated the bustling streets, his heart beat with a mixture of anticipation and anxiety. Would Rachel still remember him? Would their love withstand the test of time and the alterations he had made to their shared history? These questions gnawed at him, but he pushed them aside, holding onto the belief that their connection was timeless.

And then, in a serendipitous moment, their paths collided once again. Rachel, standing amidst the crowd, turned her head, her eyes meeting James's. In that instant, recognition and love passed between them as if no time had passed at all. The doubts and fears that had plagued James melted away, replaced by an overwhelming sense of joy and relief.

With hesitant steps, James approached Rachel, his heart pounding with anticipation. As he stood before her, he saw the reflection of their shared journey in her eyes—the trials they had overcome, the love that had persisted against all odds. In that moment, they knew that their connection was unbreakable, their love stronger than the currents of time.

Rachel reached out, her fingers brushing against James's cheek, confirming his presence in her reality. She whispered his name, her voice filled with a mixture of awe and affection. "James, you've come back to me."

Tears welled up in their eyes as they embraced, sealing their reunion with a tender kiss. The world around them faded into insignificance as they held each other, their souls merging in a timeless embrace. In that moment, the risks, sacrifices, and uncertainties were rendered inconsequential, for they had found their way back to each other against all odds.

But even in the midst of their joy, a sense of responsibility lingered within James. He knew that his actions had disrupted the natural order of time, and the consequences of his forbidden leap remained unknown. He understood that the timeline would need to find its new equilibrium, and that their love would need to navigate the challenges that lay ahead.

Together, Rachel and James faced the aftermath of James's leap, prepared to confront whatever obstacles arose. They were aware that their love had defied the laws of nature, and they were determined to honor its significance. They committed themselves to cherishing each moment, to savoring the extraordinary connection they shared, and to navigating the uncertainties with unwavering trust in their bond.

As they walked hand in hand, they began to discover the impact their love had on the world around them. The ripples of their extraordinary journey touched the lives of others, inspiring hope, healing wounds, and igniting the flames of love in the hearts of those they encountered. Their love became a beacon of light, illuminating the possibilities that existed beyond the confines of time.

James and Rachel knew that their intertwined destinies were not just meant for themselves but also for the world they inhabited. They embraced their roles as guardians of love and champions of connection, using their experiences to inspire others to believe in the extraordinary power of the human heart.

James and Rachel stood on the precipice of a future that held infinite possibilities. They had defied the laws of time, faced the risks and sacrifices, and emerged stronger in their love. Together, they would navigate the intricacies of their intertwined destinies, continuing to rewrite the story of their lives—a story that defied the boundaries of time and spoke to the eternal power of love.

As Rachel and James stood on the precipice of their intertwined destinies, they knew that the path ahead was filled with uncertainties and risks. The love they shared had defied the boundaries of time, but it also came with a heavy price—one that James was willing to pay.

In a daring move, James made the decision to take a forbidden leap back to Rachel's present time. It was a leap that defied the laws of nature, a leap that could potentially unravel the delicate threads of time and rewrite their shared history. But for James, the risks were worth it. He couldn't bear the thought of being separated from Rachel any longer.

With a mix of trepidation and determination, James harnessed the power of time travel once again. He delved into the depths of ancient knowledge, seeking the guidance and strength to undertake this perilous journey. The sages and mentors he encountered warned him of the dangers, the potential consequences that awaited him. They cautioned him about the fragility of time, reminding him that tampering with its delicate balance could have unforeseen repercussions.

But James had made up his mind. He was ready to confront the risks head-on, driven by an unwavering love that burned within his soul. He understood the sacrifices he would have to make—the potential erasure of his own existence, the rewriting of his own timeline. Yet, in his heart, he knew that being with Rachel was worth every perilous step.

As he prepared for the leap, James couldn't help but feel a mix of excitement and fear. The very fabric of time seemed to quiver with anticipation, sensing the disruption that his actions could cause. The weight of responsibility pressed upon him, but he drew strength from the love he shared with Rachel—a love that had defied the limitations of time itself.

With a final farewell to the world he had known, James took the leap. Time twisted and turned around him as he traversed the temporal currents, hurtling through the dimensions that separated him from Rachel's present. The journey was fraught with challenges and obstacles, but fueled by his unwavering love, he pressed on.

As James arrived in Rachel's present, he found himself in a world that felt simultaneously familiar and alien. He observed the changes that time had wrought—the subtle shifts in technology, the evolving landscape of the city, and the passage of years etched upon the faces of those around him. It was a world that he had only glimpsed through the words of the letters, and now he stood amidst it, ready to embrace the reality he had yearned for.

But the risks of his forbidden leap remained ever-present. James knew that the timeline had been altered, and the consequences of his actions were uncertain. He had rewritten his own existence, defying the laws that governed the natural flow of time. The delicate balance hung in the balance, and the potential for chaos loomed.

Yet, in the midst of uncertainty, James was driven by a singular purpose—to find Rachel, to hold her in his arms, and to continue their extraordinary love story. He embarked on a quest to locate her, following the threads of their intertwined destinies that still pulsed within his heart.

As he navigated the bustling streets, his heart beat with a mixture of anticipation and anxiety. Would Rachel still remember him? Would their love withstand the test of time and the alterations he had made to their shared history? These questions gnawed at him, but he pushed them aside, holding onto the belief that their connection was timeless.

And then, in a serendipitous moment, their paths collided once again. Rachel, standing amidst the crowd, turned her head

# CHAPTER 11

## THE BLOOMING OF THE TIMELESS ROSE

As the days passed, anticipation grew within Rachel's heart. The final event described in the letters—the Blooming of the Timeless Rose—loomed on the horizon. It was a rare botanical phenomenon that occurred once in a generation, a breathtaking display of nature's beauty and resilience. The event was scheduled to take place at the renowned New York Botanical Garden, and Rachel eagerly awaited its arrival.

The Timeless Rose was no ordinary flower. Legends spoke of its ethereal beauty and its ability to transcend the boundaries of time. It was said that when the rose bloomed, it held the power to unlock the mysteries of the universe, revealing secrets hidden within the folds of time itself. Rachel couldn't help but be captivated by the stories surrounding this extraordinary flower.

With each passing day, the excitement within Rachel grew. She immersed herself in the preparations for the event, reading about the history of the Timeless Rose and the significance it held in different cultures throughout the ages. Her bookstore, Past Pages, became a treasure trove of knowledge about the flower, with customers flocking to discover the tales woven into its petals.

In the midst of her preparations, Rachel found herself drawn back to the collection of letters, their words etched deep within her soul. She read them once again, finding solace and hope in the timeless love they expressed. Each letter, each emotion conveyed, reinforced her belief in the extraordinary bond she shared with James.

As the day of the Blooming approached, Rachel couldn't shake the feeling of anticipation that filled the air. It seemed as though time itself held its breath, waiting for this momentous occasion. The New York Botanical Garden buzzed with excitement, its halls and gardens adorned with vibrant displays of flowers, welcoming visitors from far and wide.

Rachel arrived at the garden early, her heart pounding with a mixture of nervousness and anticipation. The air was filled with the sweet fragrance of blooming flowers, and the vibrant colors painted a picturesque scene. She wandered through the garden, her eyes scanning the surroundings, searching for any sign of the Timeless Rose.

As she strolled along the winding paths, Rachel noticed a gathering of people near a secluded corner of the garden. Curiosity piqued, she made her way toward them, her steps quickening with each passing moment. And there, in the center of the crowd, stood the majestic Timeless Rose.

Its petals were a delicate shade of pink, seemingly infused with the very essence of time. The flower radiated an otherworldly beauty, as if it held within it the wisdom of ages past and the promise of a future yet to be written. It stood tall, defying the constraints of time, its presence captivating all who beheld it.

Rachel felt a surge of emotion as she gazed upon the blooming rose. It was a culmination of her journey—a symbol of the extraordinary love she shared with James, transcending the boundaries of times itself. The beauty of the flower mirrored the depth of their connection, and she knew that this moment held profound significance for their love story.

As the crowd marveled at the Timeless Rose, Rachel's eyes searched for James, her heart yearning for his presence. And then, in a serendipitous moment, their gazes met, locking in an embrace that surpassed the bounds of time. James, standing amidst the crowd, approached Rachel with a smile that mirrored her own.

"I've been waiting a long time to meet you," James said, his voice filled with the love and longing they had shared through the letters.

Rachel felt the weight of their journey—the risks, the sacrifices, and the unwavering belief in their love—lift from her shoulders. In that moment, they were

no longer bound by the constraints of time or the uncertainties of the future. Their love had transcended it all, and they were finally together, their destinies intertwined in a dance that defied the very laws of nature.

As they stood amidst the beauty of the Timeless Rose, Rachel and James embraced, their souls entwined in a love that had weathered the tests of time. In that moment, the world faded away, and all that remained was their unwavering connection.

The Blooming of the Timeless Rose marked the beginning of a new chapter in their extraordinary love story. It was a chapter filled with infinite possibilities, where their love would continue to flourish and evolve, leaving an indelible mark on the tapestry of time.

As the sun set over the garden, bathing the world in a warm, golden glow, Rachel and James walked hand in hand, ready to face whatever challenges lay ahead. They knew that their love was a force that transcended the boundaries of time and space—a love that would guide them through the twists and turns of their intertwined destinies.

And so, with hearts filled with hope and a love that defied all odds, they embarked on the next phase of their extraordinary journey, ready to rewrite the very fabric of time with their unwavering bond.

But their love story, interwoven with the magic of the Timeless Rose, would continue to unfold—a testament to the enduring power of love and the infinite possibilities that awaited them in a world where time held no dominion.

As the days drew nearer to the highly anticipated event, the Blooming of the Timeless Rose, Rachel's excitement grew like a delicate bud on the verge of blossoming. She immersed herself in preparations, eagerly anticipating the moment when she would witness the extraordinary flower unfurl its petals.

The New York Botanical Garden buzzed with an electric atmosphere, adorned with vibrant displays of flora from around the world. As Rachel wandered through the enchanting pathways, she couldn't help but feel a sense of wonderment and anticipation. She knew that this event held significant meaning for her own journey, intertwined with the love she had discovered through James' letters.

The whispers of fellow visitors echoed through the air, discussing the legendary Timeless Rose and its mythical properties. It was said that when the Timeless Rose bloomed, it brought with it a sense of timelessness, an invitation to explore the depths of one's heart and connect with the essence of existence.

Rachel found herself drawn to the secluded corner of the garden, where the Timeless Rose was rumored to make its grand appearance. The anticipation mounted within her, each passing moment imbued with a sense of expectation and hope. She took a deep breath, inhaling the intoxicating scents of nature, and allowed herself to be fully present in the moment.

As the sun began its descent towards the horizon, casting a golden hue upon the garden, a hushed silence fell over the crowd. All eyes turned towards the focal point—the spot where the Timeless Rose was destined to bloom.

And then, as if guided by an unseen force, the delicate petals of the rose began to unfurl. Time seemed to stand still as the flower revealed its inner beauty, its ethereal essence emanating a soft, captivating glow. It was a sight that surpassed all expectations—a true marvel of nature's artistry.

Rachel's heart skipped a beat as she beheld the magnificent sight before her. It was as if the rose held the secrets of the universe within its delicate form—a symbol of their love, timeless and transcendent. Tears of joy welled in Rachel's eyes as she realized the profound significance of this moment—the culmination of their journey, their love story blooming alongside the Timeless Rose.

And then, through the crowd, Rachel saw him—James, the dashing time traveler who had captured her heart through his heartfelt letters. Their eyes met, and in that instant, everything else faded into insignificance. The world around them ceased to exist as they gravitated towards each other, drawn by an invisible force that bound their souls.

They embraced  their hearts entwined in a love that had defied time itself. In that moment, the barriers of past and present dissolved, leaving only the unbreakable bond they shared. The whispers of their love echoed amidst the petals of the Timeless Rose, as if the flower itself bore witness to their extraordinary connection.

Together, Rachel and James stood in awe, surrounded by the beauty of the Timeless Rose and the depth of their love. They reveled in the realization that their journey had led them to this transformative moment—a union that transcended the confines of time and space.

As the sun dipped below the horizon, casting a warm glow over the garden, Rachel and James knew that their love story was forever entwined with the magic of the Timeless Rose. They understood that their connection would continue to bloom, just like the petals of the flower, offering them endless opportunities to explore the depths of their hearts and rewrite the narrative of their shared destiny.

With hearts filled with gratitude and wonder, Rachel and James walked hand in hand, ready to embrace the new chapter that awaited them beyond the garden's borders. The scent of the Timeless Rose lingered in the air, a reminder of the infinite possibilities that love and time could intertwine.

Their journey together had only just begun. Their love, like the Timeless Rose, would continue to bloom, defying the constraints of time, and carrying them into a future brimming with promise and boundless horizons.

# CHAPTER 12

## THE TWILIGHT ENCOUNTER

As the last rays of sunlight painted the sky in hues of orange and pink, Rachel stood amidst the blooming garden, her heart fluttering with a mix of anticipation and nervousness. The magic of the Timeless Rose still lingered in the air, infusing the atmosphere with a sense of enchantment. And then, like a figure stepping out of a dream, James appeared before her.

He matched the description in the letters—his eyes, warm and familiar, his presence radiating a captivating aura. Rachel's breath caught in her throat as their eyes met, and in that moment, the world seemed to hold its breath.

The crowd around them faded into the background as James approached Rachel, his steps confident yet tender. Emotion swelled within them, the culmination of their extraordinary journey converging into this singular moment. It was as if time had carved out this precise encounter, weaving their destinies together.

Rachel reached out a trembling hand, her fingers brushing against James' cheek, as if assuring herself that he was real, that he was here with her. Her voice, filled with a mixture of awe and vulnerability, broke the silence. "James," she whispered, her voice quivering with emotion. "It's you. You've come."

James smiled a smile that held a lifetime of love and longing. He cupped Rachel's face in his hands, his touch gentle yet firm, as if to imprint the reality of this moment upon his soul. "Yes, Rachel," he replied, his voice laced with affection and certainty. "I've come for you, across the currents of time."

Tears welled in Rachel's eyes, cascading down her cheeks like glistening pearls. They were tears of joy, of relief, and of the overwhelming knowledge that their connection was not just a figment of their imagination, but a force that defied the very boundaries of existence.

In that twilight embrace, Rachel and James found solace in each other's arms, their hearts beating in synchrony. It was a meeting that transcended the limitations of time and space, a union that had been written in the stars long before they even knew of each other's existence.

They spoke not in words, but through the silent language of their souls. Every touch, every shared breath, conveyed a depth of understanding that could only be born from a love that had traversed the vast expanses of time. In that moment, the whispers of their hearts merged, creating a symphony of emotions that resonated with the rhythm of the universe.

As the twilight deepened, casting a veil of enchantment over the garden, Rachel and James knew that this was only the beginning of their journey together. The challenges they had faced, the sacrifices they had made—all had led them to this point of intersection, where their paths merged into one.

With a renewed sense of purpose, they stepped forward into the unknown, hand in hand, ready to navigate the complexities of their intertwined destinies. They understood that their love was a force that would defy the constraints of time, guiding them through the twists and turns that lay ahead.

And as the stars began to sprinkle the night sky, their light shining down upon Rachel and James, they embraced the boundless possibilities that their love story held. Their encounter in the twilight became a testament to the power of destiny and the enduring strength of a love that transcends the confines of time itself.

As the last rays of sunlight painted the sky in hues of orange and pink, Rachel stood amidst the blooming garden, her heart fluttering with a mix of anticipation and nervousness. The magic of the Timeless Rose still lingered in the air, infusing the atmosphere with a sense of enchantment. And then, like a figure stepping out of a dream, James appeared before her.

He matched the description in the letters—his eyes, warm and familiar, his presence radiating a captivating aura. Rachel's breath caught in her throat as their eyes met, and in that moment, the world seemed to hold its breath.

The crowd around them faded into the background as James approached Rachel, his steps confident yet tender. Emotion swelled within them, the culmination of their extraordinary journey converging into this singular moment. It was as if time had carved out this precise encounter, weaving their destinies together.

Rachel reached out a trembling hand, her fingers brushing against James' cheek, as if assuring herself that he was real, that he was here with her. Her voice, filled with a mixture of awe and vulnerability, broke the silence. "James," she whispered, her voice quivering with emotion. "It's you. You've come."

James smiled a smile that held a lifetime of love and longing. He cupped Rachel's face in his hands, his touch gentle yet firm, as if to imprint the reality of this moment upon his soul. "Yes, Rachel," he replied, his voice laced with affection and certainty. "I've come for you, across the currents of time."

Tears welled in Rachel's eyes, cascading down her cheeks like glistening pearls. They were tears of joy, of relief, and of the overwhelming knowledge that their connection was not just a figment of their imagination, but a force that defied the very boundaries of existence.

In that twilight embrace, Rachel and James found solace in each other's arms, their hearts beating in synchrony. It was a meeting that transcended the limitations of time and space, a union that had been written in the stars long before they even knew of each other's existence.

They spoke not in words, but through the silent language of their souls. Every touch, every shared breath, conveyed a depth of understanding that could only be born from a love that had traversed the vast expanses of time. In that moment, the whispers of their hearts merged, creating a symphony of emotions that resonated with the rhythm of the universe.

As the twilight deepened, casting a veil of enchantment over the garden, Rachel and James knew that this was only the beginning of their journey together. The challenges they had faced, the sacrifices they had made—all had led them to this point of intersection, where their paths merged into one.

With a renewed sense of purpose, they stepped forward into the unknown, hand in hand, ready to navigate the complexities of their intertwined destinies. They understood that their love was a force that would defy the constraints of time, guiding them through the twists and turns that lay ahead.

And as the stars began to sprinkle the night sky, their light shining down upon Rachel and James, they embraced the boundless possibilities that their love story held. Their encounter in the twilight became a testament to the power of destiny and the enduring strength of a love that transcends the confines of time itself.

As the last rays of sunlight painted the sky in hues of orange and pink, Rachel stood amidst the blooming garden, her heart fluttering with a mix of anticipation and nervousness. The magic of the Timeless Rose still lingered in the air, infusing the atmosphere with a sense of enchantment. And then, like a figure stepping out of a dream, James appeared before her.

He matched the description in the letters—his eyes, warm and familiar, his presence radiating a captivating aura. Rachel's breath caught in her throat as their eyes met, and in that moment, the world seemed to hold its breath.

The crowd around them faded into the background as James approached Rachel, his steps confident yet tender. Emotion swelled within them, the culmination of their extraordinary journey converging into this singular moment. It was as if time had carved out this precise encounter, weaving their destinies together.

Rachel reached out a trembling hand, her fingers brushing against James' cheek, as if assuring herself that he was real, that he was here with her. Her voice, filled with a mixture of awe and vulnerability, broke the silence. "James," she whispered, her voice quivering with emotion. "It's you. You've come."

James smiled a smile that held a lifetime of love and longing. He cupped Rachel's face in his hands, his touch gentle yet firm, as if to imprint the reality of this moment upon his soul. "Yes,

Rachel," he replied, his voice laced with affection and certainty. "I've come for you, across the currents of time."

Tears welled in Rachel's eyes, cascading down her cheeks like glistening pearls. They were tears of joy, of relief, and of the overwhelming knowledge that their connection was not just a figment of their imagination, but a force that defied the very boundaries of existence.

In that twilight embrace, Rachel and James found solace in each other's arms, their hearts beating in synchrony. It was a meeting that transcended the limitations of time and space, a union that had been written in the stars long before they even knew of each other's existence.

They spoke not in words, but through the silent language of their souls. Every touch, every shared breath, conveyed a depth of understanding that could only be born from a love that had traversed the vast expanses of time. In that moment, the whispers of their hearts merged, creating a symphony of emotions that resonated with the rhythm of the universe.

As the twilight deepened, casting a veil of enchantment over the garden, Rachel and James knew that this was only the beginning of their journey together. The challenges they had faced, the sacrifices they had made—all had led them to this point of intersection, where their paths merged into one.

With a renewed sense of purpose, they stepped forward into the unknown, hand in hand, ready to navigate the complexities of their intertwined destinies. They understood that their love was a force that would defy the constraints of time, guiding them through the twists and turns that lay ahead.

And as the stars began to sprinkle the night sky, their light shining down upon Rachel and James, they embraced the boundless possibilities that their love story held. Their encounter in the twilight became a testament to the power of destiny and the enduring strength of a love that transcends the confines of time itself.

As they stood under the starry night sky, Rachel and James felt a sense of wonder and awe.

The universe had conspired to bring them together, to allow their love to flourish against all odds. They knew that their journey would be filled with challenges and uncertainties, but they also knew that their bond was unbreakable.

With their hearts intertwined, they embarked on a new phase of their lives—a journey where love and time would intertwine, where the past, present, and future would meld into a tapestry of extraordinary moments. Together, they would explore the depths of their souls, uncovering the hidden secrets of the universe and rewriting the rules of love.

As they walked hand in hand through the garden, Rachel and James felt a sense of peace and fulfillment. The Timeless Rose had bloomed, and their love had blossomed alongside it. They embraced the infinite possibilities that lay ahead, ready to face the challenges and embrace the wonders of their intertwined destinies.

And so, under the shimmering stars and the fragrance of blooming flowers, Rachel and James continued their journey—a love story that defied time, a tale that would be whispered through the ages. Their encounter in the twilight marked the beginning of an extraordinary adventure, where love would conquer all and destiny would guide their steps.

Together, they would create a love story that would transcend the boundaries of time—a story that would be etched into the annals of forgotten time, forever remembered as a testament to the power of love, the magic of destiny, and the unwavering belief in the extraordinary.

# CHAPTER 13

## UNVEILING SECRETS

As Rachel and James walked hand in hand through the garden, a mix of wonder and uncertainty filled the air. The beauty of their encounter in the twilight had left them breathless, but there were still unanswered questions lingering in Rachel's mind. She turned to James, her eyes searching his face for answers.

"James," she began, her voice laced with curiosity and a hint of apprehension. "There is so much I don't understand. How did you find me? How did you know about our connection through time?"

James took a deep breath, his gaze never wavering from Rachel's. He knew it was time to reveal the truth, to share the extraordinary circumstances that had brought them together. He spoke, his voice gentle yet resolute, carrying the weight of their shared destiny.

"Rachel, I have a gift, or perhaps a curse," he started, his words flowing like a whispered confession. "I am a time traveler. I have the ability to navigate through the currents of time, to step into different eras and witness the unfolding of history."

Rachel's eyes widened in astonishment, a whirlwind of emotions churning within her. She struggled to comprehend the magnitude of James' revelation—the notion that time could be traversed, that their connection was not bound by the limitations of a single era.

"Through my travels, I stumbled upon a collection of letters written by a man named James Thornton," James continued. "They were addressed to a Rachel, expressing a love that defied the constraints of time. It was through those letters that I first glimpsed the depth of our connection, and it was through them that I sought to guide you to me."

Rachel's heart skipped a beat as she absorbed James' words. The letters, the uncanny coincidences, the feeling of familiarity—all fell into place. It was as if the universe had conspired to bring them together, using the threads of time to weave their destinies.

But why Rachel whispered, her voice filled with a mix of awe and uncertainty. "Why did you go to such lengths? Why did you risk everything for our love?"

James reached out and gently took Rachel's hands in his, his touch a comforting anchor amidst the whirlwind of emotions. "Because, Rachel," he said, his voice steady and filled with a depth of sincerity, "from the moment I first glimpsed your name on those letters; I knew that our connection was something extraordinary. I knew that our love had the power to transcend time itself."

He paused, searching Rachel's eyes for understanding. "I left the letters for you, not only to guide you on a journey of discovery but also to protect you. Every event, every moment mentioned in those letters was carefully orchestrated to bring us together, to ensure that our love story would not be lost to the ravages of time."

Rachel's mind swirled with a mix of emotions—awe, disbelief, and a profound sense of gratitude. She marveled at the depth of James' commitment at the lengths he had gone to for their love. She realized that their connection was not just a product of chance, but of a destiny written in the stars.

As the reality of their extraordinary circumstances settled upon her, Rachel grappled with the weight of it all. The enormity of their love story, the implications of James' time-traveling abilities—it was a lot to process. Yet, amidst the whirlwind of uncertainty, there was an unshakeable feeling of rightness, of destiny fulfilled.

In that moment, Rachel made a choice. She chose to embrace the extraordinary, to trust in the power of their love, and to forge ahead on this remarkable journey. She looked into James' eyes, a mix of determination and vulnerability in her own.

"I may not fully understand all of this," she said, her voice steady, "but I believe in us. I believe in the power of our love and the connection we share. Together, we will navigate the intricacies of time and face whatever challenges lie ahead."

James smiled, relief washing over his face as he realized that Rachel was willing to embark on this adventure with him. He knew that their path would be filled with uncertainties and trials, but their love would be their guiding light.

Hand in hand, Rachel and James set forth into the unknown, ready to unveil the secrets hidden within the folds of time. They were bound by a love that transcended the ordinary, and their journey would test the limits of their hearts and souls.

Together, they would face the intricacies of time, uncover the mysteries that lay scattered across the ages, and rewrite their own story—a story that defied the constraints of time and embraced the boundless possibilities of love.

As Rachel and James walked hand in hand through the garden, a mix of wonder and uncertainty filled the air. The beauty of their encounter in the twilight had left them breathless, but there were still unanswered questions lingering in Rachel's mind. She turned to James, her eyes searching his face for answers.

"James," she began, her voice laced with curiosity and a hint of apprehension. "There is so much I don't understand. How did you find me? How did you know about our connection through time?"

James took a deep breath, his gaze never wavering from Rachel's. He knew it was time to reveal the truth, to share the extraordinary circumstances that had brought them together. He spoke, his voice gentle yet resolute, carrying the weight of their shared destiny.

"Rachel, there is something I need to tell you," he began, his voice laced with sincerity. "I am not just a time traveler. I am a guardian of time, tasked with preserving the delicate fabric of history and ensuring its continuity."

Rachel's eyes widened, her mind struggling to grasp the enormity of James' revelation. She listened intently as he continued to explain, weaving a tale of ancient powers, cosmic forces, and the unbreakable bond that had drawn them together.

"We are connected, Rachel," James continued, his voice filled with a mixture of awe and tenderness. "Through the threads of time, our souls have always been intertwined. The letters you found were not just letters from the past—they were echoes of our shared love across different eras, an unbreakable bond that transcends the limitations of time."

Rachel's mind raced, trying to process the weight of James' words. The pieces of the puzzle started to fit together—the uncanny coincidences, the inexplicable familiarity, and the unexplainable sense of destiny that had brought them together. It was as if their love story was intricately woven into the tapestry of time itself.

But why Rachel asked, her voice filled with a mix of wonder and uncertainty. "Why reveal this to me now?"

James reached out and gently took Rachel's hands in his, his touch comforting and reassuring. "Because, Rachel, our love is powerful, and it has the potential to shape the course of history. The universe has brought us together to rewrite our own story, to defy the constraints of time and create a future where our love can flourish."

Rachel felt a mixture of awe and trepidation. The weight of their connection, the responsibility that came with it, was both exhilarating and daunting. Yet, deep within her heart, she knew that their love was worth embracing the extraordinary.

As they stood amidst the garden, the fragrant blossoms surrounding them, Rachel looked into James' eyes, her voice filled with determination. "I choose to embrace this extraordinary journey with you, James. Together, we will navigate the complexities of time, uncover the secrets it holds, and forge our own path."

A smile tugged at the corners of James' lips, his eyes shimmering with love and gratitude. "Thank you, Rachel," he said, his voice filled with a mixture of joy and relief. "With you by my side, I know that we can face whatever lies ahead."

In that moment, Rachel and James made a silent vow to each other—to explore the depths of time, to unveil the secrets it held, and to let their love be the guiding force that defied the very fabric of existence.

As they embraced, their hearts beating as one, Rachel and James embarked on a journey of discovery and adventure. They would uncover the mysteries of time, face the challenges that lay in wait, and rewrite their own love story—a tale that would resonate throughout the annals of history, a testament to the power of love and the indomitable spirit of two souls entwined.

Together, they would navigate the intricacies of time, guided by their unwavering love and an unyielding belief in the extraordinary. They were determined to embrace their destiny, to unveil the secrets that lay hidden within the folds of time, and to forge a future that defied all odds.

As they walked hand in hand, Rachel and James felt a renewed sense of purpose and a deepening connection. They understood that their love was not a mere coincidence but a force that had shaped the very fabric of their existence. With each step they took, they moved closer to unraveling the mysteries that awaited them and discovering the true extent of their extraordinary love.

# CHAPTER 14

## REWRITING THEIR DESTINY

Rachel and James stood at the precipice of a new chapter in their extraordinary love story. They had unveiled the secrets of their connection, embraced the extraordinary circumstances that bound them together, and now, they were ready to rewrite their own destiny.

As they gazed into each other's eyes, a shared determination flickered between them. They understood the magnitude of their love and the power it held to transcend the boundaries of time. It was a love that defied all odds, a force that could reshape their future.

With a renewed sense of purpose, Rachel and James set out on their journey to rewrite their destiny. Together, they delved deeper into the complexities of time, unraveling its mysteries one thread at a time. They studied ancient texts, consulted with wise scholars, and explored the hidden corners of the world where time held its secrets.

As their knowledge grew, so did their bond. They became not only lovers but partners in the quest to forge a future that defied the limitations imposed upon them. Their shared experiences, their triumphs and failures, only strengthened the foundation of their love.

Along their journey, they encountered challenges that tested their resolve. The currents of time were unpredictable, and they faced obstacles that threatened to tear them apart. But they refused to succumb to the forces that sought to separate them. They fought against the tides of time, never losing sight of the love that had brought them together.

Through their efforts, Rachel and James discovered that their love had a ripple effect throughout time. The changes they made, the rewriting of their own story, echoed through the ages, touching the lives of others and altering the course of history. They became catalysts of love, spreading a ripple of hope and possibility across the timeline.

As they continued to rewrite their destiny, they found solace in the knowledge that their love was not only extraordinary but also timeless. It had the power to bridge the gaps between eras, to bring people together across the ages, and to create a tapestry of love that transcended the boundaries of time.

With each step they took, Rachel and James grew more confident in their ability to shape their own future. They embraced the unknown with open hearts, knowing that their love would guide them through the uncharted territories of time.

Along their journey, they encountered others who had been touched by the ripple of their love. They witnessed stories of lost souls finding solace, of separated lovers reuniting, and of hearts mended by the transformative power of love. Their own love story became intertwined with the stories of countless others, weaving a tapestry of hope and resilience.

As Rachel and James reached the pinnacle of their journey, they stood together at the crossroads of time. They had rewritten their destiny, creating a future that defied all expectations. Their love had transcended the boundaries of time, leaving an indelible mark on the fabric of existence.

With a final glance backward, they embraced the future that lay before them. It was a future filled with infinite possibilities, where their love would continue to ripple through time, touching the lives of those yet to come.

In that moment, Rachel and James realized that their love story was not just their own. It was a gift to the world—a testament to the enduring power of love and the indomitable spirit of the human heart.

As they walked hand in hand into the unknown, they carried with them the lessons learned, the love shared, and the unwavering belief that their destiny was theirs to rewrite. With hearts ablaze and a love that transcended time, Rachel and James embarked on their new journey, ready to embrace the endless possibilities that awaited them.

Rachel and James stood at the precipice of a new chapter in their extraordinary love story. They had unveiled the secrets of their connection, embraced the extraordinary circumstances that bound them together, and now, they were ready to rewrite their own destiny.

As they gazed into each other's eyes, a shared determination flickered between them. They understood the magnitude of their love and the power it held to transcend the boundaries of time. It was a love that defied all odds, a force that could reshape their future.

With a renewed sense of purpose, Rachel and James set out on their journey to rewrite their destiny. Together, they delved deeper into the complexities of time, unraveling its mysteries one thread at a time. They studied ancient texts, consulted with wise scholars, and explored the hidden corners of the world where time held its secrets.

As their knowledge grew, so did their bond. They became not only lovers but partners in the quest to forge a future that defied the limitations imposed upon them. Their shared experiences, their triumphs and failures, only strengthened the foundation of their love.

Along their journey, they encountered challenges that tested their resolve. The currents of time were unpredictable, and they faced obstacles that threatened to tear them apart. But they refused to succumb to the forces that sought to separate them. They fought against the tides of time, never losing sight of the love that had brought them together.

Through their efforts, Rachel and James discovered that their love had a ripple effect throughout time. The changes they made, the rewriting of their own story, echoed through the ages, touching the lives of others and altering the course of history. They became catalysts of love, spreading a ripple of hope and possibility across the timeline.

As they continued to rewrite their destiny, they found solace in the knowledge that their love was not only extraordinary but also timeless. It had the power to bridge the gaps between eras, to bring people together across the ages, and to create a tapestry of love that transcended the boundaries of time.

With each step they took, Rachel and James grew more confident in their ability to shape their own future. They embraced the unknown with open hearts, knowing that their love would guide them through the uncharted territories of time.

Along their journey, they encountered others who had been touched by the ripple of their love. They witnessed stories of lost souls finding solace, of separated lovers reuniting, and of hearts mended by the transformative power of love. Their own love story became intertwined with the stories of countless others, weaving a tapestry of hope and resilience.

As Rachel and James reached the pinnacle of their journey, they stood together at the crossroads of time. They had rewritten their destiny, creating a future that defied all expectations. Their love had transcended the boundaries of time, leaving an indelible mark on the fabric of existence.

With a final glance backward, they embraced the future that lay before them. It was a future filled with infinite possibilities, where their love would continue to ripple through time, touching the lives of those yet to come.

In that moment, Rachel and James realized that their love story was not just their own. It was a gift to the world—a testament to the enduring power of love and the indomitable spirit of the human heart.

As they walked hand in hand into the unknown, they carried with them the lessons learned, the love shared, and the unwavering belief that their destiny was theirs to rewrite. With hearts ablaze and a love that transcended time, Rachel and James embarked on their new journey, ready to embrace the endless possibilities that awaited them.

And so, their story continued, intertwined through the fabric of time. They faced the future with open hearts and a love that had withstood the test of time. Together, they rewrote their own destiny, leaving an indelible mark on the world and proving that love, in all its extraordinary forms, was the most powerful force in the universe.

# CHAPTER 15

## THE POWER OF LOVE

Rachel and James stood in awe of the boundless power of their love. Through the challenges, the uncertainties, and the rewriting of their destiny, their connection had grown stronger, transcending the restrictions of time and space. Their love had become a force to be reckoned with—a force that could shape their reality and touch the lives of those around them.

In their journey, Rachel and James had witnessed the transformative nature of love. They had seen how their own love story had rippled through time, bringing healing, hope, and joy to countless souls. It was a testament to the profound impact love could have on the world.

Their love was not just a fleeting romance but a deep connection that reached to the very depths of their souls. It was a love that defied logic and surpassed the barriers of time. Their hearts beat in unison, resonating with an energy that was palpable. Together, they were an unstoppable force.

With each passing moment, Rachel and James discovered new layers of their love. It was a love that supported them through the darkest of times, a beacon of light when the world seemed uncertain. Their love was their sanctuary, a place where they could find solace, strength, and unwavering support.

As they faced the challenges that arose from their rewriting of destiny, Rachel and James found comfort in the fact that their love was a constant. It was an anchor that kept them grounded amidst the tumultuous seas of time. They held onto each other tightly, their love serving as a guiding light in the face of uncertainty.

Their connection was not confined by the boundaries of the physical world. They had experienced love across different eras, bridging the gaps of time with a bond that remained unbroken. Their love defied the constraints of space, allowing them to feel each other's presence even when they were physically apart.

Rachel and James understood that their love was a gift—a gift that had the power to change lives, inspire others, and leave an enduring legacy. It was a love that could break barriers, transcend limitations, and ignite the hearts of those who witnessed it.

As they journeyed through time together, Rachel and James shared countless moments of laughter, tenderness, and shared dreams. They celebrated the joys and navigated the challenges with unwavering devotion. Their love was a sanctuary—a place where they could be vulnerable, where they found strength in each other's embrace.

In the depths of their souls, Rachel and James knew that their love was eternal. It would continue to ripple through time, leaving an indelible mark on the tapestry of existence. Their love was a force that would transcend generations, inspiring future lovers to believe in the extraordinary power of love.

As they stood together, Rachel and James embraced the truth that their love was a beacon of hope in a world that often seemed chaotic and unpredictable. Their connection gave them purpose, reminding them that love had the power to heal, to unite, and to create a better world.

It was their love that prevailed. It was their love that defied the restrictions of time and space, rewriting their own destiny and leaving an everlasting imprint on the universe.

With hearts filled with love and gratitude, Rachel and James embarked on the next chapter of their journey—a future where their love would continue to shine brightly, touching the lives of those around them and inspiring others to believe in the extraordinary power of love.

And so, their story continued, intertwined through the fabric of time, their love transcending the boundaries of the known and venturing into the realms of the extraordinary. They held onto each other, their love serving as their compass, guiding them through the unknown, and reminding them that with love, anything was possible.

Rachel and James stood in awe of the boundless power of their love. Through the challenges, the uncertainties, and the rewriting of their destiny, their connection had grown stronger, transcending the restrictions of time and space. Their love had become a force to be reckoned with—a force that could shape their reality and touch the lives of those around them.

In their journey, Rachel and James had witnessed the transformative nature of love. They had seen how their own love story had rippled through time, bringing healing, hope, and joy to countless souls. It was a testament to the profound impact love could have on the world.

Their love was not just a fleeting romance but a deep connection that reached to the very depths of their souls. It was a love that defied logic and surpassed the barriers of time. Their hearts beat in unison, resonating with an energy that was palpable. Together, they were an unstoppable force.

With each passing moment, Rachel and James discovered new layers of their love. It was a love that supported them through the darkest of times, a beacon of light when the world seemed uncertain. Their love was their sanctuary, a place where they could find solace, strength, and unwavering support.

As they faced the challenges that arose from their rewriting of destiny, Rachel and James found comfort in the fact that their love was a constant. It was an anchor that kept them grounded amidst the tumultuous seas of time. They held onto each other tightly, their love serving as a guiding light in the face of uncertainty.

Their connection was not confined by the boundaries of the physical world. They had experienced love across different eras, bridging the gaps of time with a bond that remained unbroken. Their love defied the constraints of space, allowing them to feel each other's presence even when they were physically apart.

Rachel and James understood that their love was a gift—a gift that had the power to change lives, inspire others, and leave an enduring legacy. It was a love that could break barriers, transcend limitations, and ignite the hearts of those who witnessed it.

As they journeyed through time together, Rachel and James shared countless moments of laughter, tenderness, and shared dreams. They celebrated the joys and navigated the challenges with unwavering devotion. Their love was a sanctuary—a place where they could be vulnerable, where they found strength in each other's embrace.

In the depths of their souls, Rachel and James knew that their love was eternal. It would continue to ripple through time, leaving an indelible mark on the tapestry of existence. Their love was a force that would transcend generations, inspiring future lovers to believe in the extraordinary power of love.

As they stood together, Rachel and James embraced the truth that their love was a beacon of hope in a world that often seemed chaotic and unpredictable. Their connection gave them purpose, reminding them that love had the power to heal, to unite, and to create a better world.

It was their love that prevailed. It was their love that defied the restrictions of time and space, rewriting their own destiny and leaving an everlasting imprint on the universe.

With hearts filled with love and gratitude, Rachel and James embarked on the next chapter of their journey—a future where their love would continue to shine brightly, touching the lives of those around them and inspiring others to believe in the extraordinary power of love.

And so, their story continued, intertwined through the fabric of time, their love transcending the boundaries of the known and venturing into the realms of the extraordinary. They held onto each other, their love serving as their compass, guiding them through the unknown, and reminding them that with love, anything was possible together, they would rewrite the narrative of their lives, embracing the infinite possibilities that awaited them. With hearts united and a love that defied all odds, Rachel and James stepped forward into the vast expanse of time, ready to create a future where love reigned supreme—a future where their extraordinary connection would inspire generations to come.

As their love echoed through the ages, they became living proof that love could conquer all, transcending time, and forever altering the course of destiny. And in their union, Rachel and James discovered that their love was not just a fleeting moment—it was a cosmic phenomenon that defied explanation, a gift from the universe that would resonate throughout eternity.

With love as their guiding light, they would continue to rewrite their destiny, leaving an indelible mark on the tapestry of time and forever celebrating the extraordinary power of their love.

# CHAPTER 16

## CONFRONTING TIME'S CHALLENGES

Rachel and James had rewritten their destiny, defying the restrictions of time and space to be together. However, as they embarked on their new path, they faced a new set of challenges. The consequences of altering timelines and the risks involved weighed heavily on their minds.

They understood that every change they made, every shift in the course of events, had the potential to create a ripple effect through time. It was a delicate balance, and they needed to tread carefully. The future they had crafted was not without its dangers, and they had to confront the challenges that lay ahead.

One of the challenges they faced was the disapproval and skepticism from those who did not understand or believe in their extraordinary love story. There were whispers of doubt and skepticism, questioning the authenticity of their connection. But Rachel and James remained steadfast in their love, knowing that their bond was unbreakable.

Another challenge was the uncertainty of the future. They had rewritten their destiny, altering the course of events, and now they had to navigate the uncharted territory they had created. The path ahead was filled with unknowns, and they had to trust in their love and their ability to face whatever challenges came their way.

As they delved deeper into their journey, Rachel and James realized that their actions had consequences not just for themselves, but for the people around them. The timelines they had altered had a ripple effect, causing shifts and changes in the lives of others. They grappled with the moral implications of their actions, questioning whether they had the right to play with time.

Their love was a powerful force, but it was not without its risks. They had to be vigilant, always aware of the potential dangers that lurked in the shadows. Time had a way of reclaiming what was altered, and they had to be prepared for the consequences that might arise.

Amidst these challenges, Rachel and James found solace in their unwavering love and commitment to each other. They drew strength from their connection, knowing that as long as they were together, they could face anything. Their love was their anchor, grounding them in the face of uncertainty.

They sought guidance from wise mentors who had knowledge of the intricacies of time. These mentors helped them navigate the complexities of their journey, providing insights and wisdom that would aid them in their quest to maintain their love against the odds.

With every obstacle they encountered, Rachel and James grew stronger. They learned to adapt, to be resilient in the face of adversity. Their love was tested time and time again, and each time, it emerged stronger, more resilient than before.

They came to understand that the risks they took were worth it. They were rewriting their own story, forging a path that defied the limitations imposed upon them. Their love was a testament to the indomitable spirit of the human heart, to the power of love to overcome all obstacles.

In their journey, Rachel and James discovered that it was not about controlling time but embracing it. They had to learn to let go of their desire for absolute control and trust in the flow of the universe. They understood that love was not something to be manipulated but something to be cherished and nurtured.

As they confronted time's challenges, Rachel and James held onto the belief that their love was extraordinary. It was a love that defied the rules of time and space, a love that had the power to transcend all boundaries. They faced the risks and consequences with courage, knowing that their love was worth it.

Together, they embraced the uncertainties of their journey, knowing that the path they had chosen was not an easy one. But they were determined to face whatever challenges came their way, united in their love and unwavering in their commitment to each other.

And so, Rachel and James continued their extraordinary love story, navigating the complexities of time and space, confronting the challenges that arose. Their love burned bright, illuminating the darkness that threatened to overshadow them. They faced the risks and consequences head-on, knowing that their love was a force that could withstand anything.

As they ventured forward, hand in hand, Rachel and James were ready to face whatever time had in store for them. They were ready to confront the challenges, to embrace the risks, and to show the world the power of their extraordinary love.

# CHAPTER 17

## A LOVE TRANSCENDING TIME

Rachel and James had faced countless challenges and overcome insurmountable odds, but through it all, their bond remained unbreakable. Their love story had transcended time, defying the limitations of the physical world and leaving an indelible mark on the fabric of existence.

As they stood at the precipice of their journey, they marveled at the enduring nature of their love. It was a love that had weathered the tests of time, growing stronger with each passing moment. The challenges they faced had only served to strengthen their connection, reinforcing their commitment to one another.

They had learned that love was not bound by the constraints of time or the limitations of the human experience. It was a force that existed beyond the tangible, weaving its way through the threads of the universe. Their love was a testament to the resilience of the human heart, an embodiment of the infinite capacity to love.

Throughout their journey, Rachel and James had witnessed the ebb and flow of time, the rise and fall of civilizations, and the passage of countless souls. Yet, amidst the vastness of it all, their love remained a constant. It was a guiding light in the darkest of moments, a sanctuary in a world filled with chaos.

The challenges they had encountered had tested the depths of their love, pushing them to their limits. But each trial they faced only served to strengthen their resolve. They had learned to trust in the power of their connection, to believe in the unwavering bond they shared.

No matter the obstacles that lay in their path, Rachel and James faced them together, drawing strength from each other's presence. They understood that their love was a beacon of hope, a testament to the enduring power of the human spirit. It was a love that could conquer all, transcending time and space.

Their love story had become a source of inspiration for those around them. It served as a reminder that love had the power to heal, to unite, and to transform lives. People marveled at the depths of their connection, finding solace in the knowledge that true love could overcome any obstacle.

In the face of adversity, Rachel and James remained steadfast in their love, refusing to let the challenges of time diminish the light that burned within them. They knew that their bond was rare and precious, a gift to be cherished and protected.

As they forged ahead on their journey, they carried with them the lessons learned, the memories shared, and the unwavering belief in the power of their love. It was a love that transcended the confines of the physical world, a love that resonated across the ages.

They knew that their love story would be remembered, not just in the annals of time, but in the hearts and minds of all those who had witnessed its extraordinary power. Their love had touched lives, brought hope to the hopeless, and inspired others to believe in the magic of true love.

Rachel and James stood as a testament to the enduring nature of love. They had faced the challenges, overcome the obstacles, and emerged victorious in their quest to be together. Their love had triumphed over time, a love that would forever be remembered as a beacon of hope, a symbol of unwavering devotion.

Their love story was not just about the two of them—it was a love story that belonged to the world. It was a reminder that love could transcend the boundaries of time, that it could conquer all, and that it could rewrite destinies.

As Rachel and James walked hand in hand into the unknown, their love burned brightly, illuminating the path before them. They were ready to face whatever lay ahead, knowing that their love would guide them through the uncharted territories of time.

And so, their love story continued forever etched in the tapestry of existence. It was a love story that defied the constraints of time, a love story that would be remembered for all eternity—a love story that would inspire generations to come.

# CHAPTER 18

## THE LETTERS OF FORGOTTEN TIME

As the final chapter of Rachel and James' extraordinary love story unfolded, their journey was reflected upon with a profound sense of awe and gratitude. The Letters of Forgotten Time had brought them together, guiding them through the complexities of time and leading them to a love that defied all odds.

Throughout their intertwined destinies, Rachel and James had faced challenges, confronted the uncertainties of rewriting their own destiny, and navigated the consequences of altering timelines. Yet, their unwavering love had remained a constant, a beacon of hope that guided them through the darkest of moments.

The letters, with their heartfelt words and hidden clues, had served as their roadmap—a connection that transcended the boundaries of time itself. Through the inked words on yellowed pages, Rachel had discovered a love that spanned centuries, a love that had the power to rewrite their own story.

Their journey had been a testament to the extraordinary power of love—a love that defied the restrictions of time and space. It was a love that had brought them together, entwining their souls across the ages and defying the very fabric of reality.

In the end, Rachel and James had embraced their destiny, taking hold of the pen and rewriting the narrative of their lives. They had forged a love story that surpassed the boundaries of the known, leaving an indelible mark on the tapestry of existence.

Their love had inspired others, shown them the infinite possibilities that waited when they dared to follow their hearts. It was a love that had touched the lives of those who had witnessed its extraordinary power, reminding them that true love was worth fighting for, even in the face of seemingly insurmountable challenges.

As the final pages of their story turned, Rachel and James stood together, their hands intertwined, gazing into a future that held infinite promise. The letters of forgotten time had served their purpose—they had brought two souls together, transcending the barriers of time and space, and allowing them to rewrite their own destiny.

The love that had blossomed between Rachel and James was no longer confined to the realm of letters and whispers through time. It was a love that had become their reality, their anchor in a world filled with uncertainty. Their connection was a testament to the power of love—a love that could conquer all, reshapes destinies, and stands the test of time.

As their story drew to a close, Rachel and James knew that their love would forever be etched in the annals of history. Their journey had been extraordinary, their love a beacon of hope and inspiration to those who came after them.

The Letters of Forgotten Time had brought them together, but it was their unwavering love and courage that had allowed them to transcend the boundaries of time and create a love story for the ages. They had defied the odds, rewritten their own destiny, and proved that true love could conquer all.

And so, Rachel and James, bound by a love that had withstood the test of time, stepped forward into their future, ready to embrace the endless possibilities that awaited them. Their love would forever be a testament to the extraordinary power of the human heart—a love that had rewritten their destiny and left an indelible mark on the world.

As the final words of their love story echoed through the chambers of time, Rachel and James embraced their love, their hearts entwined, and walked hand in hand into the unknown—a future where their love would continue to shine, a future where their love would forever be remembered as a testament to the enduring power of love.

The Letters of Forgotten Time had fulfilled their purpose—they had brought Rachel and James together, and in their union, they had created a love story for the ages—a love story that would be whispered through time, a love story that would inspire generations to come.

www.ingramcontent.com/pod-product-compliance
Lightning Source LLC
LaVergne TN
LVHW011030110826
845149LV00015B/3364

* 9 7 8 1 9 6 1 2 9 9 1 2 2 *